A Cowboy's Growing Grace

SWEET VIEW RANCH
BOOK TWO

JESSIE GUSSMAN

Contents

Acknowledgments

Cover art by Julia Gussman
Editing by Heather Hayden
Narration by Jay Dyess
Author Services by CE Author Assistant

~

Listen to the unabridged audio for FREE performed by Jay Dyess on the Say with Jay channel on YouTube. Get early access to all of Jay's recordings and listen to Jessie's books before they're available to the general public, plus get daily Bible readings by Jay and bonus scenes by becoming a Say with Jay channel member.

Chapter One

"Ezra, do you remember Terry Clomp? The girl that had the cubicle across from me?" Sondra didn't wait for his answer, which was just fine by Ezra. He had no clue who Terry was. "She told me that she and her boyfriend are finally moving in together. They've been dating for six months, and she's been staying at his place most nights. And paying for her own apartment."

She paused, and he assumed this was where he was supposed to interject some kind of sound into the conversation.

"Hmm."

"I hope it doesn't interrupt our weekly Tuesday night dinners. That's when we catch up on all the latest and watch the best series in the world, and you know what that is."

He had no idea.

"Hmm."

"Exactly. *The Bedroom and Beyond*. The actors of that show are just amazing, and the writers are perfect. Especially Bubba Goo, the most gorgeous man in the world." She sighed. Ezra supposed it was a dreamy sigh. "He's absolutely perfect, and I would just die to spend one second with him."

Sondra went on, and Ezra tried to pay attention. It was hard, because he had no clue what she was talking about. He didn't even own a TV, let alone watch one. And it seemed like every couple of weeks, Sondra's best friend changed, and he couldn't keep up.

"So," the tone of her voice shifted, and he tried to pay attention. "When are you going to invite me out? I thought you said that it was going to take you a little while to get settled in and then you were going to have me come out for a visit. I assume," her voice took on a teasing yet questioning quality, "that is so that I can look around and figure out where we'll live when we get married."

He cleared his throat. He liked Sondra, but as he looked around his office, it was primitive, and very cold in the winter, as was the rest of the house. And the entire ranch actually. Considering that it was in North Dakota, everything was cold in the winter. But they were just coming out of the long, cold snowy season, and he really didn't have an excuse.

He liked her, but the idea of having her on the ranch for a couple of days, or more, made him want to turn and run in the opposite direction. He would have to entertain her, lead her around, be by her side every waking second, and he didn't have time for that.

"Well, I want to make sure that things are ready for you," he hedged. There was something wrong with him. It wasn't Sondra. All of his siblings teased him that he was never going to get married. Maybe that was the reason that he'd not shut her down the first time she tried to talk to him. Or maybe it was because he knew they would be moving soon and didn't think they would stay together.

Whichever it was, he felt like a heel. Probably because he was one. He should just tell her now that he didn't want her to come out and that maybe they should start seeing other people. And she'd blindsided him when she assumed they were going to get married. Except, she was already talking again by the time he got his mouth open.

"That's so sweet of you. That's one of the things I love about you. You're so protective, just like the hero in my favorite movie." And then she went off on a tangent describing her favorite movie.

He started to sigh and managed to stop himself just in time, before he did it into the mouthpiece of his phone.

She was still describing the first act, as far as he could tell, when his brother Asher walked into his office.

He held up one finger, indicating to Asher that he would be with him in a moment.

He waited for Sondra to take a breath.

"I'm sorry. I need to go."

"Aww," she pouted. "All right. I'll text you later and let you know how the tournament turns out. And I'll send you pictures of the shoes that I bought. You can let me know which ones are your favorites. I'll be sure to pack them when we nail down a date."

"All right," he said.

They hung up, and Ezra stared at his phone for just a moment. He really needed to tell Sondra that they just weren't going to work out.

"She trying to come out again?" Asher asked with a perception that irritated Ezra. He was really good at seeing things that needed to be done, figuring out the best ways to do things, and working his butt off.

People, women in particular, seemed to be beyond his ability to figure out.

A person would have thought, considering that he was the oldest of twelve children, and that he had six sisters, including two twin sisters who were barely two years younger than him, he would have a little bit of something figured out.

But his brain just didn't seem to work the way that it needed to in order to understand the gentler sex.

Actually, he didn't find females to be all that much more gentle than males.

But his grunt seemed to be answer enough, because Asher grinned, picking up the stapler that was on Ezra's desk and straightening it up before he set it back down. "You know, if you're going to get married to her, you probably ought to look forward to seeing her and try to figure out how you can be together, not to mention, you should enjoy her company."

Right. He probably knew that. But he was content to call her his girlfriend, talk to her once in a while, or maybe just a little bit more often, and live in one state while she lived four states away.

Yeah, that probably wasn't the best foundation for a marriage.

"You don't usually have trouble getting things done," Asher commented, lifting his brows and looking down his nose at Ezra.

The look made Ezra push away from his desk and stand to his feet. Asher was eight years younger than he was and a half an inch shorter. With a conversation like this, Ezra felt like he needed every inch of his height.

"And I'll get that done too. You're right."

"Yeah. If you can get a word in edgewise. Never met anyone who could talk as much as Sondra can." Asher lifted one brow. "Even Joanna," he said, referring to their second youngest sister. Joanna was number eleven of twelve, and Ezra figured that she probably had to do a lot of talking in order to get noticed

But Asher was correct. Even Joanna couldn't outtalk Sondra.

Or maybe it was just that Joanna said things Ezra was interested in or could get interested in. The latest TV show or the perfect style of shoe was not something that would help him run his ranch and therefore was not something about which he had much to say.

"Excuse me." The door pushed open. Alaska, whom he had just hired to be his personal assistant, popped her head in the door.

"Come on in," Ezra said, figuring that whatever Asher had to say could wait.

"I just wasn't sure whether you wanted me to file those folders in alphabetical order or by date," she said, one hand reaching out to twirl the earring in her lobe.

She had piercings in her upper ears as well, but she didn't seem to mess with those. That was something he'd noticed in the last four days she'd been there.

"File the ones with the names on them in alphabetical order. File the ones that have general information by date," he said, remembering that she was working on the bulls he'd used in his herd for the last four years, as well as the different updates that they'd done to the ranch so far, since they had bought it almost a year prior.

They had been going to buy it almost eight years before, but things had gotten held up when they tried to sell their ranch in Wyoming.

If they hadn't, he probably wouldn't have gotten entangled with Sondra.

He tried to push that thought out of his head. He wasn't through with Sondra, and maybe things would work out after all. Since all the problems were on his end, he was responsible for trying to fix them.

He knew there were defects in his personality, and if Sondra was willing to put up with him, he should put more of an effort into their relationship. So far, she hadn't complained, but he could see a lot of room for improvement.

"Ezra?" Alaska's voice came again.

"Yes?" he said, noting that she was playing with her earring again.

"You told me to tell you when the kids were sleeping because you wanted to go over what my duties were going to be. They're sleeping."

He kept himself from smiling. For some reason, he had been looking forward to talking with her. They had hosted a wedding on short notice on the ranch, and she had spearheaded everything. He'd been impressed by her organizational skills and her ability to jump in and do whatever needed to be done, while rolling with the things that didn't work out. She didn't get upset, and while she was understandably hassled, it wasn't in a grumpy or short-tempered way. He admired her.

She obviously made some interesting choices in her life, but a person could argue that so had he.

"Let me finish talking to my brother, and I'll come find you."

The door closed behind her, and Ezra noticed for the first time that Asher had a smirk on his face.

"What's so funny?" he asked, making sure he was standing to his full height as he crossed his arms over his chest.

"Are you really hiring her?" Asher said, rather than answer his question.

"I said I would. She needs a place to stay where she'll be protected."

"You realize that whoever's after her is probably some kind of drug dealer?"

"That's kind of judgmental, don't you think?"

"Sometimes judgmental is accurate. I'm not maligning her character, I'm just asking. After all, my family lives and works here. And

I have a vested interest in keeping them safe. I thought you did too." The smirk had vanished from Asher's face, and his expression was serious.

None of them ever took the safety of their family for granted, and for the Clybourns, family had always come first. Even ahead of helping people, although they'd never shirk from doing that either.

"You're right," he acknowledged, knowing that sometimes a person earned a reputation, and they looked it. "But she has two small children and nowhere to go. Someone was threatening her, just threats. I said she would be safe here, and I believe she will be."

"But will we?"

"Do you want me to tell her to go?"

"I just don't trust the way you were looking at her."

"What do you mean?" Ezra's eyes narrowed. He really had no idea what his brother was saying.

"You were looking at her the way you should be looking at Sondra, except you look bored out of your mind when you're on the phone with Sondra. I don't even have to hear any of the conversation. I just look at your face, and I know it's her."

Ezra took two steps and turned toward the window, looking out on the green fields of the ranch where horses grazed in the distance, separated from a field of cattle by a section of fence. They worked long and hard to get that fence up. And they had a lot more to put in. But the ranch was looking a lot better than it had been when they moved in. Which was the idea. Ford Hansen along with Travis Baker had invested in them, and he didn't want to let them down.

"I was concerned that you have her here because you feel something for her. And not because you're trying to keep her safe. And sometimes that means that you forget what your actual responsibilities are."

"You're talking like that's happened before. We both know it hasn't."

"Just because it hasn't happened before doesn't mean there won't be a first time."

Ezra jerked his head, without turning around to look at his brother. Those words were true. It was an arrogant man who thought that something could never happen to him. Ezra had been around long enough to know that about the time he thought he was immune to something, he would come down with it.

"What do you suggest I do?" he asked, without turning around. He wanted to be humble enough to ask his younger brother for advice and to take it seriously. In his mind, part of being a good leader was humility.

Chapter Two

E zra had just said to himself that he had been looking forward to talking to Alaska. Maybe Asher knew something that he himself didn't know yet. Although, everything that was serious and intentional about him screamed that Asher was absolutely wrong. Sure, he had been looking forward to talking to Alaska, but it had been because she had done such a great job with the wedding. Not because he had any personal feelings toward her. After all, he had just been on the phone with his girlfriend. He wouldn't be thinking about Alaska or doing anything inappropriate with her. He was known for his principled way of life.

"I suggest you let her go. You can't help everyone. Just like you can't adopt every stray puppy that comes along."

"Alaska is a stray puppy?" he said, pleased that his voice sounded level. He hadn't expected Asher to say that. He didn't want to let her go. He wanted to...keep her. The word "forever" came into his head, but he pushed it aside. Surely she didn't mean that much to him. That was just one of those fluke words.

Plus, Alaska was hardly the kind of girl that a man like him would keep forever. Not that he was better than she was, just that they had made completely different decisions in their lives, and before that, they had been brought up in completely different ways.

Still, the idea of putting her out as Asher suggested rubbed him exactly the wrong way.

"See? You don't want to do it. That tells me everything I was saying before is absolutely accurate."

"I wouldn't want to put anyone out without any prospects for a job. Especially someone who wanted to work."

"I think it's for the best interest of our entire family for you to let her go."

"Why is that?" he asked, hedging to give himself some time. He needed to marshal his arguments. Or he could just agree with Asher. Was the fact that it was so difficult for him to come to terms with the idea that he needed to let Alaska go, just more proof that Asher was correct?

"A woman like that has done drugs. You can tell by looking at her."

"You're judging her tattoos?" Ezra personally did not like them. But that was just personal preference. She had tattoo sleeves up both arms and something inked around her neck. There wasn't anything on her face, but she did have a lot of piercings.

Ezra had none. No ink. No tattoos. No piercings. That was by deliberate choice. But just because a person had them didn't mean that he was going to judge them for it. Just as he hoped that someone with a lot of tattoos and piercings would not judge him for not having any. The way he saw it, it was a two-way street.

The only thing that might change that was the fact that the Bible clearly commanded for a person not to have any piercings or tattoos. It was an Old Testament command, one made under the law. He wasn't a Bible scholar, and he didn't know whether that was something that no longer applied, or whether it still did. But if it did, he supposed it would apply to all tattoos and all piercings. Even the typical piercings that most ladies, even Christian ladies, had in their earlobes. If piercing was wrong, it was wrong across the board. If it wasn't, then it wasn't across the board. There were no exceptions. The Bible certainly did not give any of those.

As for him, whether it still applied or not really didn't matter. He'd rather be safe than sorry and had zero desire to put graffiti on his skin or holes in his body.

"If someone has used drugs, they have friends who use drugs. They have a dealer. They might even have a pimp."

"She doesn't have a pimp," he broke in immediately.

"How do you know?"

He pressed his lips together. He supposed he didn't. It was just... "This is Sweet Water, North Dakota. Not New York City or Los Angeles. There are no pimps."

"I'm pretty sure that you're wrong about that." Asher's words were cool, calm, and not inflammatory at all. He was making a logical argument, and Ezra had to admit, he was winning. It hurt to be beaten by his younger brother, especially one that was so much younger than him. Compared to him, Asher was still wet behind the ears.

"I might be. But that's no reason to throw her out."

"I didn't suggest you throw her out. I said let her go. We can certainly help her find another job, find another place to stay. We don't have to endanger the entire family or bring drugs onto our ranch. We're struggling enough as it is."

Ezra kept his mouth closed. Ford and Travis had invested heavily in the Sweet View Ranch. But because of the issues with getting permits, and the way the years had dragged on, their investment had not shown much fruit. Ezra had not wanted to ask for more. He wanted to be able to make things work with the money that they'd been given.

Beyond that, he wanted to make sure Ford and Travis saw a tidy profit, and that he was able to get the ranch to be solely in the Clybourn family.

That seemed like a pipe dream, since he wasn't even sure whether he was going to be able to make it work at all, without even paying them back.

"I can't disagree with you."

"Then you see the wisdom in not having another problem come on the ranch!"

"She's not a problem. She's a person. With two small children."

"That's another thing. With little kids, she can't work nearly like someone who doesn't have children. She almost needs someone to watch those children."

Ezra couldn't argue with that either. She hadn't been able to talk to him until the children were sleeping. That's what she had just stuck her head in the room about.

"I heard her say that the kids were sleeping so she could talk to you."

It was like Asher had read his mind.

"Ezra. Usually you make really good decisions. But my eyes almost popped out of my head when you brought her here. And now, you're acting like she's going to stay...forever."

"Not forever. Just until she gets back on her feet."

"Do you want to run the ranch into the ground? That's what's going to happen if you take up every stray person and animal that comes along. Or even one. We just don't have the resources right now. I want to help people as much as you do. I do! We just can't right now. A drowning man has to save himself first. He can't go and help others when he can't keep himself above the water."

"Let me think about it," he finally said after staring out the window at the horses, not really seeing them. He shoved his hands in his pockets and turned around. He'd found that it was usually best to present a confident front, but he didn't want to mix confidence with arrogance. And as much as he didn't want to hear what his brother was saying, he pretty much knew he was right.

"Listen, I know you don't want to hear it. I know that, and you gotta believe me, my heart bleeds for her just as much as yours does. But we have to take care of family first. If she was your wife, it would be a completely different story. But she's not. And right now, we just can't afford to take on someone who can't pull their own weight, but is going to drag down other people, and potentially bring drug dealers and who knows what all else out to the farm. We just can't."

Ezra nodded, his lips pressed tight together, his hands fisted inside of his pockets. He didn't say anything, because there wasn't anything he could say that would be a good argument to what Asher had just pointed out. They would take care of their own, and if she were a part of the family, either by birth or by marriage, they would absorb her and take care of her. But she wasn't.

"Ford asked me to take care of her as a personal favor. I couldn't tell him no. Not after the investments that he's made in our ranch and after the money we owe him, and he's been patient enough to wait."

"Taking care of her is one thing, keeping her forever is something else. We've had her for a few days. When the danger, or whatever the problem was, blows over, she needs to go."

He did not agree. He couldn't. But he nodded anyway. "I'll see what I can do."

Asher's eyes narrowed. He knew that was not an agreement. But he also knew that if Ezra gave his word, he would keep it. If he said he would think about it, he would. And he intended to. Because Asher had great points.

However, he had told Ford that he would take care of her, and that was his word.

"Maybe you need to keep your word somewhere else," Asher finally said before he lifted a brow, waiting for Ezra's chin jerk before he turned around and walked out the door.

He closed it carefully behind him. He hadn't walked out angry and did not slam it. There was no way that they could make the ranch work if everyone got mad every time someone disagreed with them. They could have disagreements, they could have discussions, they could even have intense discussions, where someone was sure that their way was the right way, but at the end of the day, they all had to be able to get along, jump in, and pull together. It was the only way the ranch would work.

Ezra had preached that to his brothers and sisters since they had started talking about trying to make this go. It was the way his parents had run their family. Ezra wasn't sure that parents could have twelve children and have the entire family get along without preaching some such thing. Disagreements were okay, and anger, in its place, was not necessarily terrible either. But selfishness and anger that a person could not get a hold of, that drove a person to do things that were unkind or unbiblical, was not acceptable.

He took a deep breath and blew it out slowly. He needed to talk to Alaska, and he wasn't sure what he was going to say. That, and the conversation that he had with Sondra, weighed heavily on his mind. It also irritated him, because he should be thinking about the ranch, about the weanings that were coming up, about the price of cattle, and how it was down. They'd held off weaning their herd for as long as they could, hoping the price would go up. But it hadn't, and they were scheduled to work cattle the next day.

What was he going to tell Alaska?

He still hadn't figured it out when a knock sounded at the door.

"Come on in," he said, trying to make the tension release out of his shoulders and put the problems out of his mind.

His sister Phoebe walked in. Phoebe was the older of the twins which came in line directly after him. They were just about two years younger than he was, and he'd grown up with them dogging his every footstep.

When he'd been thinking about going to North Dakota to try to make a go of the Sweet Water dude ranch, he wouldn't have done it without Phoebe and her twin Priscilla coming with him.

Since their parents had died, they had banded together to raise the younger children. Phoebe had put off marriage and lost a long-time boyfriend because of her move.

Priscilla had been married, but it hadn't worked out.

As soon as she saw his face, her brows came down.

He should have known that he wouldn't be able to hide anything from Phoebe.

"What's wrong?" She stepped in, putting both hands behind her and leaning against the door, pushing it closed carefully, all the while studying his face.

"I told Ford Hansen that we would give Alaska a place to stay safe. But Asher feels like not only whoever is after her could be a problem at the ranch, but he also feels like...like she's been with some unsavory people and she might bring those to the ranch as well. He thinks it's unfair of me to keep her here and wants her to go."

"Well, he's not wrong." Phoebe's words were matter-of-fact. He wouldn't expect anything less from her. Priscilla was a little more dreamy, with her pie-in-the-sky attitude and her tendency to look at life through rose-colored glasses. That tendency had faded a bit with the dissolution of her marriage.

"I know," he said, striding around his desk but too restless to sit down. "But that's not why you came in here. What do you need?"

"I wanted to make sure that we had all the vaccines and wormer we need for tomorrow. I was doing some inventory and have to run into town for some groceries and supplies. I could pick those things up if you need me to."

"Let me check with Tobias," he said, naming the brother who typically was in charge of the health of the cattle herds.

He pulled his phone out and sent off a quick text.

"It's not like you to waffle about decisions. But you look kind of torn up about this one."

"I guess I just feel bad for her. She's had a rough life. You can tell that by looking at her. But Asher is right. A person who has those kinds of friends could bring those kinds of friends around and could jeopardize everything that we're working for."

"What? Do you think we're all suddenly going to become drug users?"

His lips did not twitch, but he allowed the humor to show in his eyes. "I might be a little concerned about you. You always did waffle a bit."

That time, his lips did curl up. Just one side.

"Right. You know I always have a tendency to walk on the wild side." She rolled her eyes. Of all of them, Phoebe was the one who was content to be at home, to be...boring. It bothered her some, he knew. That she wasn't more exciting, didn't have any desire to leave the ranch or to live a big life. She just wanted to serve her family, and she took a lot of flak about it from friends who thought she was way too old to be still living at home. That she had too much talent to waste it on working for her family.

He couldn't disagree about her talent, but he did disagree with everything else. Phoebe was doing exactly what she thought God wanted her to do, and that was never a waste. Even if it didn't look like what the rest of the world thought a person was supposed to be doing. Just because society said a person had to move out of their house and go to college at eighteen and then get a job, work for ten years before getting married, buying a house, and having kids...if that was still what the world said, that didn't mean that if they lived according to the world's standards rather than the Bible standards, a person wouldn't miss out on a lot in life that was more important. It was always better to follow the Bible.

His phone buzzed, and he looked down. "He sent me a list. I'll copy it and send it to you."

"All right. Thank you." She turned to go. But then she stopped and turned around, with her hand on the knob. "Ezra?"

"Hmm?" he said, already trying to think about how many weanlings they would have and which of the three places he'd gotten prices from would be the best ones to send them to.

Chapter Three

"We can't save everyone. You know that." Phoebe's face held concern.

"I know."

Boy, did he ever. But he had always been grateful that he had grown up with a stable home. Parents who loved him. Parents who stayed together. A mom and a dad in his house. So many of his friends didn't even have that much. It seemed like a small thing, but it was a major part of a person's childhood, whether or not they had a mom and dad.

Then, when his parents died, and his younger siblings were left without parents, of course he had stepped up for them. And he'd often thought that if his siblings hadn't had him or the rest of their family, who would have taken care of them? Would someone else have stepped up?

He could see that with Alaska. There she was, a young, single mom, who hadn't had great guidance in her life. She didn't seem rebellious or exceptionally defiant. She just hadn't had the opportunities, the circumstances that he had. How could he not help her?

Except, if his siblings didn't want him to, if they argued that they couldn't afford to, he could hardly argue back.

Phoebe left, and he sent the list he had promised, then shoved his phone back in his pocket, wrapping his hand around his neck. Walking back over to the window where he looked back outside. He loved that view, loved seeing the horses in the pasture, loved seeing the cows grazing, the buildings in the distance, the busyness as people walked across the parking lot, from one implement shed to another, someone got a lawnmower out, someone else had a tractor torn apart, with pieces lying on a piece of cardboard, and feet sticking out from underneath the underbelly of the machine.

He probably should go out and help. There were so many things to do, he almost didn't know where to start. Two of his other brothers were fixing fence, and his sisters were painting the interior of the bunkhouse where their guests for the summer would hopefully be staying.

A crash jolted him out of his contemplations. He turned facing the door, listening. It sounded like there was a struggle going on, and he strode to the door, yanking the knob open.

The filing cabinet that had been next to the wall had been completely knocked over, and papers were scattered everywhere, but that wasn't what caught his attention immediately. It was the fact there was a man in the room, and he had Alaska in a headlock with her body pressed to his, and her chin lifted at an unnatural angle as he tightened the pressure, growling something in her ear.

"What's going on?" he said, raising his voice just a bit but still sounding calm and in control. The man didn't seem to have a weapon, other than himself.

The man's eyes jerked up. "This little girl is mine. And she's coming with me."

Ezra hadn't been around too many people who did drugs in his life before, but this person had a wide-eyed look that said he might be on some kind of speed-type drug. Ezra wouldn't even know what kind of drug that was, other than it made people think that they were invincible, and they would do stupid things, like break into a ranch and grab a woman right out of the living room, surrounded by people.

"I think if you have to put your arm around her and strangle her in order to get her to go with you, it's probably best if she doesn't."

He didn't know how to reason with someone like this. He wasn't even sure a person could. When someone was on drugs, they weren't reasonable.

It was quite possible that this person had other problems. His clothes were ragged, dirty, and his hair stood out in all different angles. He had as many tattoos as Alaska and almost as many piercings. He was skinny, a typical look for a drug user, but it was the eyes, those wild, crazy eyes that didn't look like they had a soul behind them, that made the hair on the back of his neck lift, and his heart beat hard.

Someone like that would be capable of anything.

"Get out of my way. We're leaving."

"No!" Alaska said, her word cut off as the man jerked his arm tighter, cutting off the air and pinching her windpipe closed.

"Let go of her," Ezra said. He wasn't sure how the man would react, but he pulled his phone out of his pocket and dialed 911. He didn't try to talk, knowing that they were required to look into any call. Hopefully they'd send someone out, and soon. He left the phone on, hoping that the dispatcher could hear that there was something going on.

"I think you might be high," he said, trying to make his voice sound calm, although he didn't think there was much hope in de-escalating the situation.

"I might be. You should be too. Life is better when you're high," the man said, laughing with a manic sound that sent chills down Ezra's spine.

He swallowed, his throat tight. Alaska's face was red, and Ezra hated to do it, but he figured he didn't have much choice.

Dropping his phone to the ground, he strode forward, grabbing the man's hand and yanking it, hoping that the suddenness of his move would keep the man from stiffening his arm and keeping it around Alaska's throat. He was worried she was going to pass out, or worse.

It worked, and the man loosened his grip enough that Alaska was able to get free, but Ezra was distracted because as he moved away, she started to follow, and he reached out to grab her as the man's fist connected with the side of his face.

Pain shot through his body, and the force of the blow made him stumble back.

He might have taken longer to recover, but the man lunged toward

Alaska, and Ezra's sole focus was on keeping him from grabbing her again. The man was stronger than he looked, as skinny as he was. Maybe it was the drugs, but he was afraid that he would end up killing Alaska without even realizing it.

Ezra couldn't remember ever hitting anyone in his life before, but he balled his fist up, like he did it every day, and slammed it as hard as he could into the man's left eye. Ezra was not exactly a lightweight, having worked on the ranch all of his life, but the man barely blinked.

It had to be the drugs. Ezra followed the first punch with an uppercut to the jaw while the man's attention was diverted from Alaska to him.

"Get out!" Ezra said firmly to Alaska, figuring that even if he couldn't subdue the man, at the very least Alaska and her kids would be safe.

But instead of listening to him, Alaska turned to the man, punching him in the stomach before he grabbed her hair.

Adrenaline had dulled the pain in his face somewhat, and Ezra had an odd feeling of being outside his body as he hit the man in the stomach again and tried to get another blow in while working to figure out what in the world he could do to make the man let go of Alaska's hair.

She screamed, the man yelled, and Ezra punched him twice more, hoping to either knock him out or make him let go.

After he hit him in the stomach for the second time, the man screamed, an animal-like sound that conveyed anger and rage, and ran at Ezra.

It was intimidating, but Ezra stepped forward into it, deflecting the man's fist while grabbing a hold of his arm, and moving it, trying to pull it back and hold it behind him. They wrestled for a bit, with the man grabbing hold of Ezra's leg and Ezra leveraging that to his advantage by pressing into the man rather than away, and they both tumbled to the floor.

They scuffled there, with Ezra's larger size, and perhaps his experience in wrestling steers, allowing him to get on top of the man, his hands pressed against the floor while the weight of his lower body kept the man still under him.

"Get off me!" The man followed that with a string of curses, spewing language out of his mouth so filthy it almost made Ezra's hold loosen, just to hear it.

He made sure to stay well away from the man's mouth, because he wouldn't put it past him to bite, and with the enraged, incoherent way the man was, if it were possible, he would bite clear through.

"I told you to get back," he snarled at Alaska, angry that she had put herself in harm's way after he had freed her.

"I'm calling 911," she said, completely ignoring his words and pulling her phone out of her pocket.

"I already did."

He could just hear his brothers now. This would be great press for the ranch. Exactly the kind of press they did not want. And he had to admit that Alaska looked like she had done this type of thing before.

Even while he thought that, there was a vulnerability about her that pulled his heart.

This man could be him, although Ezra didn't have as much compassion for him. Alaska, at least, was trying to get her life turned around. This man was trying to keep her from it. Ezra couldn't help but want to help her. Of course.

But his siblings would never let him do that now. They would want her gone, as fast as possible. They would want to help, but from a distance. It would jeopardize everyone if they kept her here, and Ezra couldn't argue about it. They were all right.

"What's going on?" The door burst open, and Asher came in, those words tumbling from his lips before he'd even taken a step inside.

He laughed. A humorless huff of air. "You're taking care of him the same way you took care of Caleb when you guys wrestled when you were kids."

"Why fix it if it ain't broke," Ezra said, grunting a bit as the man struggled underneath him.

To his side, he could hear Alaska speaking calmly into the phone. Again, like she had done it before.

"I always hate it when I'm proved right." There was irony in Asher's tone, and he didn't need to say anything more.

"I hear you," Ezra said. "Before you start gloating, do you think you can give me a hand, so I can get up?"

"Seems to me like you've got things under control. Kinda looks like you were about to take a nap or something." He strode over, smirking. "It's not too often I see my big brother lying around on the floor. Let me enjoy it for a moment before I give you a hand."

"Shut up, and help me," Ezra ground out, annoyed. "Why couldn't Phoebe have come back in? At least she would give me a hand before she told me all the things I've done wrong."

He had to admit, there were times women were much better than men. This was one of those times. A man was far more likely to make fun of someone than to help them, especially if they didn't look like they needed help. But he didn't want to lie on the floor forever, and the guy was still high. And dangerous.

"He's on something. Be careful," Ezra said as Asher got closer.

"Yeah." Asher didn't say anything more, but his lips were drawn and flat, and Ezra didn't need to hear him say anything more, or hear his thoughts, to know what he was thinking. Everything that he had said in the office, not even ten minutes ago, had been borne out in the last five minutes. And he would waste no time in telling Ezra that Alaska needed to go, today probably.

It wasn't that his family didn't have a heart, he knew it. Still, after this, Ezra would have to agree with them. What if one of his sisters had been in the room? What if the man had tried to take them, or worse, what if he had had a weapon?

"This is going to look great on the headlines for the ranch," Asher muttered as he pulled some binder twine from his back pocket, and Ezra grunted. So many times, he shoved twine in his pocket, intending to throw it away, and ended up carrying it around with him the rest of the day. This was not the first time that it had come in handy at some point.

It was, however, the first time that they had used it on a human.

He could hear sirens in the distance as he got gingerly up, and then they helped the man to his feet.

"Watch it," he said to Asher as Asher allowed his ear to get dangerously close to the man's mouth. "I wouldn't put it past him, in the state that he's in, to try to bite that off your head."

"A decent sort of fellow, you say," Asher muttered. Obviously disgusted with the entire thing.

He supposed both of them were thinking about how this was going to affect the ranch, not the animals they raised, or the horses they trained, but the dude ranch they were hoping to open. Asher had been right about having the wrong kind of people showing up here. It would be terrible for business.

"I'm so sorry." Alaska came over and stood beside him, looking up with concern on her face. "I'm sure that the police are going to want to ask you some questions, and then... I can get my kids up and leave."

"No."

"Yeah, that'll be good."

Asher and he spoke at the same time.

He set his jaw and turned to give his brother a stare. "She's not leaving."

"She said she was."

"No."

"Don't be stupid," Asher said, irritation heavy in his words.

He knew he was being ridiculous. Alaska should go, she even said she would. But he couldn't... He couldn't even explain why he didn't want her to go. There was just something about her.

"It's okay, Ezra. I appreciate you taking a chance on me. But Asher is right. If I stay, they might still come back, thinking they can take me. Or convince me to go."

"No. I gave my word to Ford. You'll stay."

"It's not safe for you. For the rest of the people here."

"We'll talk about this later," he finally said as a siren got louder and then shut off, and there was a pounding on the door before the police walked in, guns drawn.

"This is a new low," Asher muttered, throwing a dark look at Ezra before putting his hands in the air, facing the cops.

Chapter Four

Alaska couldn't believe she had brought this kind of danger down on a good family. She also couldn't believe how big the family was. And every single one of them was in danger because of her.

"All right. That's it for now." The officer clicked on his iPad and then looked up at her. "Thanks for answering our questions."

"Sure," she said. Once upon a time, she would have run from the police, but she hadn't done anything wrong, and she wanted Rex out of her life. The officers had said they would put a restraining order against him, but she knew if he was on drugs, it wouldn't make a difference. When a person was on the kind of drugs that he used, he wasn't afraid of anything. Not a restraining order, not anything any sane person would be terrified about.

She had no idea what she was going to do or where she was going to go. She couldn't go back to Travis, although he and Ellen had been kind to her. Maybe she could drop her babies back off. Her heart clenched as she thought of little Alice, barely two months old, and of Eugene, who was two. But she could be separated from them, and at least they would be safe.

She would also have less worries, because she wouldn't have to try to figure out how she was going to work around them. It had been perfect here at the ranch. She could work while they were sleeping, and some of the things she needed to do she could do while they were awake.

She had thought this was her dream job. But Rex had made sure to ruin it. Although, she thought maybe Ezra was the only one who was completely on board with her being there. One of the other brothers, Asher, had seemed to not want her at all. Not that he had been unkind, because he hadn't. He just seemed to know the danger she represented, and while it pained her to admit it, he had been right.

"All right. If we need any more information, we'll give you a call. I have your number." The officer held out his hand, and after blinking and choking back her surprise, Alaska took it and shook. She wasn't used to the police considering her to be one of the good guys.

She kind of liked that feeling.

She wanted out. Truly, but it was hard. Once a person had fallen to a certain point, pulling themselves up became difficult, if not impossible. Especially without help.

She bit her lips and checked her phone to see if her children were up. She couldn't believe they had slept through all of this, but normally when they didn't get a morning nap, they both slept for two or three hours in the afternoon. They were at the far end of that, but Alaska considered it the one good thing that had happened to her today: her children had taken good naps.

As she walked out of the kitchen where the police had been questioning her, her eyes met Ezra's, as he stood by the mantel in the living room, leaning against it, his arms crossed over his chest.

Two of his brothers stood in front of him, and his sister Phoebe was also there.

His other brothers had come and gone, and a couple of his sisters had run over to check things out. Everyone had gone back to work, because as one of them said, "There's no point in standing around waiting for the police to do their jobs when there's work waiting."

It was a new kind of idea to Alaska. Where she came from, everyone stared at the police until they left. And then they talked about it, good and bad, for days afterward.

The idea that work might interfere with what usually proved to be pretty good entertainment was novel.

"Do you have a minute?" Ezra said, pushing off from against the mantel as his siblings turned to see who he was talking to. Disapproval seemed written on their faces when they saw it was her.

"Sure," she said softly, feeling defeated and not having the energy to hide it.

"My office?"

She nodded and then followed as he led the way. Another time or another place, she might have admired the broad shoulders, long legs, the confident stride, the way his arms swung a little at his sides, like he knew what he was doing and who he was.

She envied that to a point. She had gotten out of where she was, because she returned to the religion of her childhood. Too late to undo a lot of the mistakes—she understood that just because she became a Christian didn't negate the fact that she would be reaping what she sowed for a long time.

It also didn't change the fact that she was determined to sow new crops. They wouldn't help her today, most of them anyway, but eventually, down the road, she would have a better harvest than what she could currently expect.

Still, she hadn't gotten to the point where she had the kind of confidence that Ezra displayed. Maybe she never would.

He held the door, waiting for her to walk through it before he closed it behind her.

She put her arms around her waist and squeezed tight. Knowing that it wasn't exactly a confident look, but her stomach felt like it was going to run away, and she felt like she needed to hold it in.

"You can sit down if you want to," Ezra said, and his voice held compassion. He could be very commanding, and he often was. In the few days that she'd been here, she heard him issue orders with a rapid-fire, almost drill sergeant mentality. But he always used a softer, kinder tone on her. It had annoyed her, as much as she had appreciated it. After all, she didn't want to be treated with kid gloves. She was strong, capable, and could take care of herself.

Except, she kind of liked that he seemed to want to take care of her. Right now, she definitely wanted to let him.

"No thank you. I understand what you need to say. I brought this to your ranch, and everyone is in danger because of me. Thankfully, he was only after me."

"We're not thankful about that." He interrupted her, and gave her a look, before he turned around and walked over to the window. She'd seen him stand there multiple times. It seemed to be where he went when he needed to think. He crossed his arms over his chest and stared out.

"All right. Whatever. I know I have to go."

She didn't need this to drag on. In fact, she didn't wait for him to say anything but turned and took two steps toward the door.

"Wait," he said, his voice commanding. And then it softened with the request, "Please?"

It was the "please" that did it for her. That and the little bit of time that she spent with this family, she'd come to respect and appreciate them. It was easy to see that they were hardworking and did not expect anyone to hand them anything. She could admire people who worked for what they had. She hoped to be one of them. She didn't want to keep them from being successful, and she definitely didn't want any of them to get hurt.

"I heard bits and pieces. I understand that Asher, especially, wants me to go."

"He's the most vocal. The other ones will be okay whatever we decide."

He had said "we." Like she had some say in it.

"I don't see that there's any other decision to make. Unless you have a ranch somewhere far away, like Florida?"

He snorted. "I can't say that might not be an idea that's crossed my mind in the middle of the North Dakota winter."

He was laughing? Not really. His lip turned up, and it was more emotion than he typically displayed.

"I take it that's a no," she said, unwilling to be drawn into a lighter moment. This was serious. This was her life. This was the life of her children.

"That's a no. This is the place we have. We sold the ranch in Wyoming, and this is all we have."

"Well, it's more than I have," she said, starting to turn back around.

"Do you want to listen to what I have to say?"

"I can't imagine that you're going to say anything that is going to change things."

"Well, this is a setback for the ranch. I don't need to talk to you about the financial situation, but we're new, and it's going to take a little while until we're solid in that area. Not gonna lie."

"I didn't think you could."

"I think any man can do pretty much anything, so keep that in mind. It's only through the grace of God that man will not fall into sin, especially when he's tempted."

She didn't say anything. She hadn't been a practicing Christian long enough to know exactly what he meant by that.

"We do have choices."

"All right." She took a breath in and let it out, trying not to show her impatience. If she was going to have to leave, it would be nice if she could get her small amount of stuff packed before the kids woke up from their naps.

"You have two children to look after."

"I know." She tried not to be sarcastic. She had borne those children. She knew better than anyone she was responsible for them.

"I know you've given them away before, trying to get a start, and I'd like to keep you together with them if I can."

"That's a big responsibility. And it's not really yours."

"I know. But... I can't really give you reasons why, but I want to help you."

"That is very noble. It's probably so that you can pat yourself on the back and feel like you've done your good deed for the day. Or the year, if you help me."

"Or a lifetime."

His words were soft, and she didn't catch them at first. Then her ears perked up, and she tilted her head.

"A lifetime?" She couldn't even think in terms of a lifetime. She was still thinking in terms of her next meal. Of what meal she was going to feed her children.

"That's how long you can stay."

"How?" she said, wondering if she missed something. She could stay for a lifetime? Easy. She could do that. She had nothing else pressing at the moment. No one else who wanted her, nowhere else to go. She could be their servant for a lifetime, if they just let her stay.

She opened her mouth. "You want me to work without pay? I'll do it. Want me to commit to stay here forever? I'll do it. You want me to... sign something in blood? Give me the paper. Show me a knife. I'll do it."

"Will you marry me?"

Her mouth fell open, and her heart stopped beating. Her eyes searched his. Was he serious?

"Is this some kind of cruel joke?" she finally said, when she was able to get her mouth to work again.

"No. It's the only way. If you're my wife, everyone will rally around you. They'll protect your children, and you'll be part of the family. It doesn't matter what happens then, because family is more important than the ranch."

His face was impassive, and she couldn't read a thing on it. He hadn't said a word about wanting to marry her, and why would he? He'd known her for all of four days, and they'd barely spoken. Plus, she wasn't exactly the kind of woman that a man like him got married to.

"So you're just going to marry me until I'm safe, and then...we get it annulled?"

"No. Marriage is for a lifetime."

He said those words like there was no arguing with them. When she knew full well that most marriages did not last a lifetime. In fact, she knew of only one or two that had actually lasted a lifetime. That just didn't happen in modern times anymore. Marriages didn't last.

Of course, she would fight for her marriage. She would make sure it lasted. If that's what he wanted.

Except, it couldn't possibly be.

"So, let me get this straight. You want to marry me. A real marriage. Even though you barely know me. In fact, do you know my last name?"

"Slessing."

"Right. You processed my employment papers."

"And I remembered."

She almost thought a bit of humor crossed his face, although she couldn't be entirely sure. She couldn't believe he could find anything about the situation funny. But then again, he held the upper hand. Except... She did. He was the one who had asked her.

She could say no. It was her choice.

"All right. You get credit for that." It was reluctant, but she supposed it couldn't be all about her. He was giving her the upper hand, and she could take it and wield it over him, or she could do what he was doing and be gentle with her power.

It seemed like when someone got a little bit of power, they liked to lord it over people. Goodness knew she had that done to her often enough. But she could be different. She could be...gracious with her power.

"Thank you," he said, irony in his voice, but his face once again impassive. "You need to think about it carefully. I don't plan on getting married twice."

Chapter Five

"Well, if you're looking for a pure, virgin bride, remember I have two children." Alaska wanted to tell Ezra about the other things that she had done, but this was the best opportunity she had... ever. She didn't want to talk him out of it.

"I know you have children."

"Well, there's a lot of other things you don't know." She couldn't keep herself from saying it. If he was looking for a lifetime love, he needed to look for someone else. She was hardly lifetime love material.

"Do any of them matter?" he asked, like she would seriously tell him.

"I've done some pretty awful things for money. I don't know what matters to you." That was a flippant answer and not the truth. He was a righteous man, someone who valued purity and honesty and integrity, and all those other things that she wasn't. She knew those things would matter to him.

"The only thing that matters is that you're not married to somebody else. It would be illegal in that case for us to get married. The only other thing that matters to me is if you're going to keep your word or not. Because if you're not planning on keeping your word, I'd rather you didn't give it to begin with."

Was he for real?

"You don't want to know about the things I've done? You don't want to know about the fact that the father of my children was married when I slept with him? You don't want to know that I used to sell myself in exchange for drugs?"

She wanted to slap her hand over her mouth. The things she hadn't wanted to tell him had come out. In the form of questions, sure, but they'd still come out.

He hadn't flinched when she spoke. She'd seen his eye twitch, but he hadn't changed his position.

"But that's not who you are anymore." His words were a statement, not a question, and she found herself nodding in agreement. That was how she felt about it. That wasn't typically how other people felt about her. They saw her past and considered her a part of it.

And she couldn't fault them for that. A person was a product of their past. The things that they had said, done, and lived, watched and read, those all went in and made a person.

When Jesus came into a person's life, he could make them new. She'd experienced that.

Even though she still had guilt over the sins of her past, the way she lived, the things she'd done, she knew that when God looked at her, He didn't see those things.

Sometimes it was hard to believe, but she knew it to be true. Jesus had paid the penalty for those sins, and in God's eyes, she was just as pure as the man standing in front of her. The thing was, the rest of the world would look at them differently. She couldn't believe he didn't.

But there couldn't be anything else. "What benefit is this to you?"

"I told you. I can't explain why."

That confused her. She wasn't used to people doing things out of the goodness of their heart. The reaction of his siblings made a lot more sense to her. While she knew that Asher was probably the only one who really didn't want her, and the other ones would probably allow her to stay, Ezra actually wanted her. He wanted her so much he was willing to marry her—a lifetime commitment, real marriage, marry her—in order to keep her.

"I don't get it. I don't understand what you see in me. Why you'd want to help me. Why you'd go to such great lengths to...have me stay."

He lifted his shoulder, like it didn't matter. Like it wasn't a big deal. Like he wasn't...giving up everything for her. Which basically he was.

"Aren't you going to want to get married sometime? Didn't I hear a rumor about your fiancée coming to visit?"

At the mention of his fiancée, he had more of a reaction that he'd had over anything.

"I knew it. You have a fiancée. I don't understand." She was leaning toward the idea that she had to begin with, that this was some kind of cruel joke that he was playing. But what she couldn't figure out was why. It seemed like a sadistic game. And Ezra did not seem like a sadistic kind of person.

"I'm sorry. I can't explain. But the offer is there. It's up to you whether or not you want to take it."

She closed her mouth. She wasn't going to get an explanation. And she wasn't going to get any declarations of undying love either. She was hardly in the position to hold out for more. She almost laughed at the thought.

How could she justify the idea that she could have gotten someone like Ezra to marry her, raise her children, and make a lifetime commitment to her, and decide not to do it because he didn't give her a declaration of undying love? Yeah. That was smart.

Yeah. She couldn't imagine anyone ever saying that. At any point.

"All right. I'll do it. But the kids are going to be up soon." She had no idea what time frame he was thinking about.

"When I spoke to the police, they said they were going to try to hold the dude as long as they could, but they weren't entirely sure that they could get a judge to set bail high enough to keep him. Obviously, he's a danger to you. We're going to get a restraining order, but the sooner you and I get married, the safer you'll be."

She couldn't believe that he was going to marry her, just to protect her and keep her safe. Couldn't believe that he cared that much about her.

"We've only known each other four days. I don't understand why you're doing this."

"I'm not sure why either. Except... I need to."

Well, that was fair. He kept saying he had no idea. Maybe he was being honest. She couldn't remember ever doing anything without reason. Nothing this big.

"How soon works for you?" he said. Turning from the window, walking over to his desk, he picked up his phone and presumably pulled up his calendar.

"This job is the only thing I have on my schedule. So, whenever you can spare me, I can do it."

He stopped swiping and clicking for a moment and looked at her over the top of the phone. Lifting one brow, and maybe it was humor in his eyes, she wasn't sure.

"All right then. We're working cattle tomorrow, so we'll do it the day after. I'd like to get a preacher, but if we can't, we can go to the courthouse in Rockerton."

"All right." He wasn't exactly asking for her approval of his plans, but she felt like she should give it anyway. She supposed her saying she would marry him was approval enough.

Maybe she should be offended on some level. Like she should get a say, but he hadn't asked her what suited, and she'd said anything. So he went ahead. It was the kind of commanding nature that he had. She should...appreciate that, she supposed. Maybe along with that commanding nature came a protective streak, that apparently included her.

"You're going to take care of my children, right?"

"I was assuming we would do that together."

"I mean if anything happens to me. Like a father. If we're married, you said for a lifetime, and I'm assuming that the children are included."

That was a lot, but she didn't want him to be unsure about what she meant. She meant everything. He was going to do anything the kids needed.

She appreciated that he didn't answer right away with something flippant. His face looked thoughtful, like he was processing what she said to make sure he understood.

"I'll provide for them. I'll be their father. The same as if they were mine. Is that what you are asking?"

"I suppose."

"Nothing is going to happen to you. But in the case that, down the road, at some point, God takes you home, I will raise the children. They're mine."

She had not put a father's name on the birth certificate. The father of the children had been married to someone else. She...regretted that probably more than anything.

"What?"

It amazed her that he must have seen that on her face. She thought she had been hiding her feelings well. Apparently not well enough.

"Nothing."

He didn't seem like he believed her, but he didn't push.

"All right, then we'll plan on taking care of this the day after tomorrow. When I've called the pastor and figured out a time, I'll let you know."

She nodded, feeling the buzz of her phone and pulling it out.

"Eugene is up," she said.

"All right. I'll work on getting those papers put back where they belong. If you want to just focus on cooking supper and getting ready for tomorrow, that's fine. I'll... I'll be moving into the little house with you."

She wanted to get offended that he hadn't asked if it was okay, but it made sense. If it was a real marriage, an actual marriage, they should probably live together.

A little slice of panic went through her as she turned and walked toward the door. She didn't know how to be married. She didn't know how to be a wife. She had no clue on what she needed to do. How to make this last. How to...make him happy. Was that even her job?

She stopped, just before she opened the door, and turned back around. He still stood behind the desk, his hands planted on either side of it, his head hanging down, almost as though he felt defeated.

She hated that the idea of marrying her made him look so...beaten down. She should tell him that she changed her mind. That she wasn't going to go through with it. That he was free. If she were a better person, maybe she would.

"Are you okay?" she asked softly instead. Maybe she could work her way up to being a better person.

His head lifted, and his face looked every bit as determined as it had before. "Yes."

"Is there... Is there someone I can talk to? I... This might sound funny, but I'm not sure how to be a wife, and...I feel like you deserve a good one."

That time, both corners of his mouth turned up, and she would definitely term his expression a smile.

"Yeah. I think there are some ladies who might come over...even this evening if you want them to."

"I don't need them that fast, although...I guess the sooner I get started, the sooner I can work on getting better."

"I'm sure you're going to be fine. This isn't something you have to get worried about."

"You don't understand. I don't have anything to bring to you; you're giving me everything, a home, a chance at a new life, a place to work, a dad for my kids, and I... I don't have anything to give in return." She didn't have to go into all the details about the life she led before and how she was bringing more baggage than anything else into this marriage. She didn't want to be a taker. She didn't necessarily want to be a giver, although maybe that should be her goal, but she wanted their relationship to be more equal. Not with him doing all the giving and her doing all the taking.

"I'm sure things will even out over the years. That's what a relationship is. Give-and-take, and it's not always equal or even. It's just that we both do whatever we need to in order to keep our marriage together. Strong."

"I don't really have any examples of a strong marriage."

"My parents had a strong marriage." His voice sounded a little far away, like he was thinking about days past. Better days. Happier days. Days with people he loved.

Would he ever think about the days they had like that?

She hoped so. She hoped that even though she didn't really think it was her job to make him happy, she hoped that between the two of them they could create happy memories.

Then she thought about the farm, and the problems on that, and realized that some of their memories might be really bad to start out with, especially if they lost the farm. Maybe once they were married, she would ask if there was anything she could do in order to help save it. That could be her first contribution to their marriage.

Chapter Six

Was there a right way to break up with someone?

Ezra pushed his hammer, with the claw gripping the wire, with one hand to stretch it, while he pounded his staple in with the other.

He stopped, standing back and looking at his handiwork.

It was easier to fix fence when there were two people, but he wanted to get this up before they brought the herd in to do a herd check and weanings the next day.

Everyone had been scrambling to make sure things were prepared, and despite the chaos of the morning, he wanted to do his part.

Somehow, they needed to do a herd check, and he needed to get ready to be married the next day. And in the meantime, he needed to figure out how to break up with Sondra.

He had hoped that he would be able to run to Rockerton first thing in the morning, but the courthouse probably didn't open until nine, and by then, they were always knee-deep in whatever ranch work they had for the day.

He hated to just skip out. Even though he would be fine if one of his brothers had something come up and absolutely couldn't make it. He didn't figure any of his siblings would care, but it wasn't the responsible thing to do, and Ezra always did the responsible thing.

Except, getting married after knowing someone for four days was hardly the responsible thing.

Lord?

The more he thought about it, the more he thought that he'd been reading about Hosea that morning in his Bible for a reason. It seemed like God was speaking to him, as he knew He often did through His Word.

He put a hand on the fence and looked out over the fields. Cattle dotted the green grass with black spots as the rays of the sun cast long shadows and daylight faded.

It was a beautiful time of day, one of his favorites. Probably his absolute favorite, after sunrise. There was nothing he liked more than to stand outside with a cup of coffee in his hand, watching the sun come up, thinking about the day, meditating on the scripture that he'd read before he even left his room.

He supposed his life would be changing if he had children to take care of. A wife to...protect. At the very least.

Typically, once he made a decision, he didn't waffle back and forth about it, but this decision was so out of line for him, so out of the ordinary for anything that normal people did, that he couldn't help but wonder if it maybe wasn't a rash one. And one that he would repent in leisure over.

"Hey, Ezra."

He turned, seeing his sister Priscilla walking toward him. She carried a tumbler, which he was sure had cold water in it, and he smiled.

"Always happy to see you, especially when you're bringing me a drink."

"I see how you are. You need me to be doing something for you in order for you to want to see me."

He knew she was teasing, and he laughed, but he sobered immediately. "I don't want to be like that."

"I wouldn't tease you about it, if you really were."

He nodded, but he figured there probably were times where he was more concerned about getting things done and ordering people around than he was about the mental and spiritual health of his siblings.

"Mom and Dad were always really good about that. They made us work, and they made us work hard, but they always took time to make sure that we were okay. Not physically, but...that our hearts were right."

"And you do that too."

"But not as good as they did."

"We have a tendency to remember people, especially people who passed away, with rose-colored glasses. We forget the bad, and we just remember the good. Which I think is good, but you're holding yourself up to an impossible standard. Mom and Dad were not perfect."

"I know they weren't. I just feel like... I'm not doing a good job."

"You having second thoughts about getting married?"

"Was it that obvious?" He took the tumbler she handed him and drank all the water around the ice and wiped his mouth with the back of his hand. "Thanks."

"You deserve it. You had quite a day."

"Yeah. It's not every day that you have the police descending upon your house and interrogating you."

"I was thinking it's not every day that you decide to get married."

"Now I need to figure out how to tell Sondra. What's the right way to break up with someone?"

"Probably not by telling them that you're getting married the next day to someone else." Priscilla smiled, but there was a bit of sadness in her eyes.

"That's pretty bad, isn't it?"

"Yesterday I would have said that you and my ex had absolutely nothing in common. But...that's a little closer to cheating than makes me comfortable."

"Ouch."

"Sorry."

"No. I would far rather you be honest with me, and help me fix my faults, than ignore them, and pretend they don't exist."

"You don't have very many. And I mean that honestly."

He appreciated her saying that. He also appreciated her insight. She had been married, and she had the scars from that marriage. She would have insight that he didn't. He appreciated her sharing it with him.

"I think it's too late for me to do it the right way then."

"Yeah. You and Sondra probably never should have gotten engaged to begin with."

"We never did get a ring."

"Why did you ask her anyway? I never really thought you liked her that much."

"She asked me. I don't even think she asked me. At least, I wasn't thinking of it as a marriage proposal. She just said in one of her rambles that we should get married. When she stopped to take a breath, I agreed with whatever it was she said, and the next thing I knew, she was announcing to the world that we were engaged. I...figured I might as well marry her as anyone and let it go."

"You didn't stop to see what the Lord thought about that?" Priscilla asked, sounding as though that were the obvious thing for him to do.

"No. I... I guess I just didn't think about it. I mean, I wasn't exactly thinking about getting married, and I wasn't thinking about asking her, I wasn't thinking about answering her either, since she did the asking and the answering, and I just didn't argue. It...just kinda happened."

"I don't think I would've ever looked at you, as commanding and purposeful as you are, and thought that some woman would have tricked you like that."

"Well, I kinda did want to get married." He set the hammer down on the back of his four-wheeler and then lifted his hat and ran a hand over his hair, scratching a bit where the rim pressed against the scalp.

He settled his hat back down on his head.

"You're lonely? That's crazy in a family as big as ours. And as unusual as our family is. Typically everybody goes their own way, but we all just kinda hang out together."

"We work together. We all had a purpose. And the ranch was big enough for everyone. And Mom and Dad made sure that everyone had something to do that matched their interests."

"Yeah."

That was another wise decision his parents had made. He had a commanding attitude, and his dad had taken him along, showing him how to manage things. One of his brothers had a head for numbers, and a couple of his sisters had worked in graphic design. They all did the grunt work on the ranch, but some of them liked it more than others and spent more time on it. Everyone pitched in where they were needed. Sure, there were fights and disagreements, but his parents had lectured, and Ezra had taken up the drum about being able to disagree without fighting or hating each other.

"So are you going to seriously go ahead with the wedding so soon? It's going to be a lot anyway, with trying to work the herd tomorrow. That's always a big day."

"Yeah. I think the sooner we get it done, the better. It will solidify Alaska's position here."

"You mean, it will make her part of the family and we'll be obligated to take care of her."

"I guess if you want to look at it like that. I just know you will. Even though we're not married, I assume everyone knows the plan is there, and you'll still take care of her."

"We will, but she'll still be in danger from...whatever friends she has."

He heard how Priscilla said "friends." She didn't mean it in an unkind way, but she didn't necessarily consider someone who wasn't out to help a person, but was rather intent on harm, as the man was this morning, a friend.

"Yeah. That would probably be the only reason I feel like there's a rush. She... She's trying to do right. And I know that there are places that will help her. But there's no better place than right here. Am I wrong?"

"No. You're absolutely right. She's just not the kind of girl that I ever pictured you ending up with. But I know that if you marry her, you'll stay with her until you die. Do you... Do you really think it's a good idea?"

She was playing to the doubts that were already in his mind. Not necessarily because of the person Alaska was, but because he didn't know her that well. How much more afraid must she be? She didn't know him any better, and he could overpower her at any time. He was a good bit bigger than she was, and definitely stronger.

"You know, she kept asking me why, why was I asking to marry her, why did I want to. And I couldn't answer. I don't know that I can answer you either. I just... I was reading in Hosea."

"Oh."

He smiled, loving that Priscilla knew exactly what he meant when he said he had been reading. Hosea had been commanded to take a prostitute as a wife and bring her home.

That wife had left him, and he'd gone back for her. He didn't necessarily think that Alaska was going to leave him, but he could see some similarities. Not that she was a prostitute, necessarily, but that a person would have thought that Hosea would marry a godly woman, as befitting his position as a prophet. But God had someone else in mind for him.

Their love story wasn't necessarily a great one, but the applications were there, and it just felt like a nudge from the Lord.

"I don't know how else to explain. Other than I just feel like...like it's what the Lord wants me to do. It felt right when I thought about it and even more right when I suggested it to her. I figured if she disagreed, that was out of my hands, and what kind of woman agrees to marry a man that she only knew for four days? I really didn't think she'd consent."

"But she did."

"Yeah. And here we are." Him with the problem of what to do about Sondra, and this feeling that what he was doing with Alaska was exactly right, coupled with the nerves that clenched and unclenched his stomach.

"Do you still feel like this is what God wants you to do?"

"I do." He knew that without a shadow of a doubt. It was so out of line for him, so unusual, that it almost could only be from the Lord. He certainly had thought that. He was almost forty years old and had yet to even have a serious enough relationship to be engaged, other than Sondra, and he wouldn't have termed their relationship serious. They'd only been out a couple of times. They mostly saw each other at church and community functions where she came over and hung out at his side. It...was a relationship that didn't feel right to him.

It was crazy, because Sondra was the "right" kind of girl, at least according to the way anyone would see it, looking at them. She was like him. Had been raised the way he had, although not in as big of a family, but in a small town, with most of his values and morals.

Alaska... She was as different from him as night was from day.

"Are you sure that you're not just attracted to her because she's different than you are?"

"I can't say that the thought hasn't crossed my mind. But I've met a lot of people who are different than me. And I've never felt drawn to them before. I've never felt like I needed to ask them to marry me before."

"They've never been in this situation before."

"That's true."

"But, if you are still certain that this is what the Lord wants you do, then I think you need to go through with it."

"Thank you. I appreciate that." He paused for a moment, and then he said, humbly, "Can I ask you something?"

She lifted her head to the breeze, cooler now that the sun was down, although it wasn't fully dark. The sky was ablaze with orange and reds and pinks, and they had shifted to stand shoulder to shoulder, looking at the colors blaze overhead.

"Sure. Ask away."

"I'm going to probably sound weird, but I'm serious. I... I know I need to break up with Sondra, like you said. And I really would appreciate any advice or help that you can give me. I... I'm not good at this type of thing. And it will be tempting for me to say, I never really agreed to marry her in the first place, but that doesn't seem like the best way to go about doing it. But at the same time, I don't want to hurt Sondra's feelings, but I want to balance that with the fact that Alaska is going to be my wife, and I don't want her to feel like I catered to Sondra and didn't care about how she felt. That I put more thought into making sure Sondra didn't get upset than I did about how Alaska might feel about me being so considerate to Sondra, when she's the one I'm marrying. If that makes sense."

"You want to make sure that she knows that she is the most important one to you."

"Exactly. Sondra I care about, but Alaska... She's going to be my wife."

"Just because she's going to be your wife doesn't mean you have any special feelings for her. You seem to be struggling about that."

"Well, our society sometimes has a twisted view of what love is. If I say that I love her, people might get the idea that I'm infatuated with her or that I have feelings that...I really don't have. But if we're talking about love the way God commanded us to love someone, where we do it with our actions, or love is patient, love is kind, love does not envy, love does not boast, it's long-suffering, not proud... I mean, I can say that I love her now."

"Yeah. I understand that, but I can see how you would hesitate. You wouldn't want anyone to get a mistaken idea."

"Yeah. Including Alaska. I... I can promise to love her, but I can't promise to have feelings that may or may not ever come."

"Do you think that's fair to her?"

"Dad told me once that you have feelings sometimes, especially when you're a teenager, that's where I was. I was probably fifteen. He said they feel strong, but feelings lie. He said that marriage isn't supposed to be about feelings. It's supposed to be about treating someone else the way God wants you to treat them, even when you don't feel like it. Especially when you don't feel like it."

"You know, sometimes I think we were really blessed to have so much time with Mom and Dad. I feel a little bit bad for the younger kids, who didn't get to spend as many years with them as we did. But they have you."

She smiled at him, looking over, like she admired him. He supposed it was a pretty big deal, considering that she was his sister and had grown up with him, and knew him almost as well as anyone did. She knew his faults and foibles, and she admired him anyway. That made him feel pretty good.

"So, to answer your question, I suppose there aren't supposed to be feelings, if I asked the right way."

"Maybe. But I do think that there's some kind of feeling, something that makes one person special, more than another person, and makes you think to yourself, 'I really want to spend more time with this person. I enjoy them.'"

"I always thought that was because they made you better. That you should want to spend time with someone who makes you a better person. Who challenges you to grow, who encourages you, who believes in you. Who can see the potential that God put in you and wants to help you touch the world with it."

"That's a pretty tall order."

"You don't agree?" Maybe he was pie-in-the-sky. He usually had both feet planted firmly on the ground, but sometimes he could have some lofty ambitions. He always thought that his wife would be someone... Even if she wasn't quite the wind beneath his wings, as the cliché went, someone who was wind to him, the same way he would be wind to her. Maybe that was asking too much of someone.

"I think it sounds really good in theory. Sometimes in practice, I think in a relationship especially, people get jealous of each other. They each want to be the top person. And they keep score. You know, 'I did more for you than you did for me, so now you owe me.' Because, to make someone better, sometimes it takes a level of sacrifice that a lot of people aren't willing to give."

"Well, even if just being around her makes you better. You know? Like you see them doing something, and it inspires you to up your game. Not in a competitive way, but because you know that what they're doing brings them closer to the Lord, and when you're around people like that, they have a tendency to inspire you to want to be the same."

"Yeah. I can see that."

They were quiet for a bit, and then he prodded her gently, "Suggestions about Sondra?" He really had no idea. He knew he needed to call her. Knew he needed to let her know that the future she was planning wasn't going to happen. That was definitely a harder call than what he wanted to have to make, but sometimes a person just had to do the hard things. And this would be one of those.

"No. I guess the best thing to have done would have been to have done it back when she first started saying that you are engaged. The second-best thing would have been to have done it before you decided you were going to marry someone else. Now... I guess I would call her and at least talk to her on the phone. It would be easier to send a text, but that seems a little..."

"Low class?"

"Yes. For lack of a better word. It just seems inconsiderate."

"All right."

The sky held just a little bit of color now, and the cows had made their way over to them, so the munching sound of the cows eating combined with the music of the wind through the grass, gently blowing.

"Well, I'll leave you then, since I assume you're going to do that now?"

"Yeah. Might as well get it over with."

"Let me know how it goes," she said, and then she walked away, slowly through the grass, as though she were thinking about what they were talking about. Or maybe other things. Like her children.

Chapter Seven

Ezra said a short prayer, and then he took his phone and pulled up Sondra's contact, hitting the button to call her.

"Ezra!" she said, picking up the phone in the middle of the first ring, like she had been waiting for him. "I was just going to call you. I have so many things to tell you. First of all, you would not believe what happened on *The Bedroom and Beyond*."

"Sondra."

"No. I'm serious. I need to tell you this."

"Sondra, I need to talk to you."

Either she missed the serious note in his voice, or she chose to ignore it. "Well, you can tell me in a minute, but first, I know you didn't catch the show last night, and it was insane. First of all, they killed off the best character. That's Joe. You do know the best character, right?"

"I can't get married to you, Sondra."

"And then, at the funeral, Luke took off with her—" There was silence for just a second, and then she said, "What?"

"I can't get married."

"Of course not. Not today. Not this year. Because I don't have enough time to plan a wedding, but we can set a date for next year. I'm so glad you finally want to set a date. Why didn't you just say so?"

"No. No date. We can't get married."

"Can't?"

"Can't. I... I'm breaking up with you." He had never said that before. And it didn't sound good. He didn't plan to ever use those words again, and they came out of his mouth, off his tongue, harsh and discordant in the night air. Not even the munching of the cows in the grass could make them sound sweet, or right, even though he knew they were words he needed to say.

He should never have allowed her to think for more than two seconds that they were going to get married. Priscilla was absolutely right about that. But that was his stupidity, and while he hoped to never have that kind of issue again, at least he felt like he was a little smarter than he used to be.

"You can't break up with me. Because I'm breaking up with you. I never liked you that much to begin with, and I was only marrying you out of pity. You're weird, first of all. You never talk, secondly, and you don't talk about your feelings even if you could talk. It's annoying. I don't know how I put up with you for as long as I did. Also, you're bossy. Just in case no one ever told you, although surely someone has. Because it's a huge defect in your character. And I very much question your character. In fact, I think you've been sleeping around. I'll definitely be sure to tell everyone that when they ask why I broke up with you." She gave a small huff. "Goodbye."

Ezra held the phone to his ear for just a few more minutes. She had hung up on him. After accusing him of cheating on her.

That wasn't exactly how he intended for that to go.

But his purpose had been accomplished. They were officially not together anymore.

He hadn't exactly wanted it to happen quite like that, but he supposed that it was better that they were broken up than that she had somehow tried to talk him into staying together. But considering how terrible he was, she certainly wouldn't have wanted to do that.

He would have laughed at the absurdity, except the conversation didn't leave him feeling very good. In fact, he felt worse than he could ever remember feeling since his parents' funeral.

I suppose this is what I get for allowing it to go on instead of stopping it. I took the easy way out, and this is payment, right, Lord?

There was a little bit of a shift in the breeze, and while he knew it wasn't God speaking, it still made him smile. Remembering God's still, small voice speaking to his chosen man, Moses.

Ezra had never gotten to the point where he wanted to speak to God, and he had to admire Moses's courage in wanting that to begin with.

Knowing that he'd regret what he'd done with Sondra for a long time, he stayed until full darkness had descended, praying that he would be a good husband, that things would go well with the weanings in the morning, that no one would get hurt. That he would be able to be a father, a *father*.

When he thought of the example of his dad, he felt intimidated, but he knew that his dad had to start somewhere too.

Maybe a relationship like his parents had would never happen for him. He could hardly imagine Alaska and him having the kind of love that seemed to flow effortlessly between his dad and his mom, but he hoped for that. Whatever God gave him was what he would take, and he would try to be happy with it. Since that was what God wanted.

He secured his tools, got on the four-wheeler, and rode slowly back to the house, just one more day as a single man.

Chapter Eight

Alaska picked up the full clothes basket, put it on one hip, and grabbed Alice and put her on the other.

"Be careful, Eugene. Sit down on your butt and slide down." She watched as Eugene obeyed, sitting on his rear and sliding down the steps. Eugene was too little to be able to climb down them the regular way, and there was no way Alaska could carry the baby and the basket and Eugene too.

Going up the stairs, she could put Alice in the basket and then hold Eugene's hand.

She sighed. It was almost dinnertime, and she was exhausted. Ezra had said that while he could use her help outside, the kids would need to stay out of the way, and they weren't old enough to know where they could be safe and stay there. So, he'd asked if she would stay inside and cook lunch so that Claudia, who usually did the cooking, could go out and help.

She had been more than happy to. She figured the more she did, the more she'd start to fit in with the family.

He also mentioned that if she wanted to, she could move his things over to the small house. The twins, Phoebe and Priscilla, as well as Claudia and Asher, all lived in the big farmhouse.

Ezra had moved out of the small house for her, and some of his things weren't even unpacked in his bedroom.

She hadn't quite recovered from the day before, and every time she went down the steps, she looked around, making sure that no one had come in the house that wasn't supposed to be there.

Her heart fluttered, and her hands sweated as she followed Eugene down the stairs.

This was the sixth or seventh trip she made, and Alice was getting heavy.

There was still one more load.

"Good job, Eugene. Now stand up so Mommy can finish coming down the stairs." She didn't expect anyone to come. Rex was the only one who wished her harm, other than Chalmer, who had threatened her at times, but she didn't really think Chalmer would follow through. He was...not a nice person, but he wasn't prone to violence either.

Plus, he wasn't quite as far into the drugs as what Rex was.

She had seen how they wrecked a person's life. She wished that she could have believed without experiencing, but there wasn't any way to go back and redo the past, so what she had to do was try to take the lessons that she'd learned and put them to good use.

That reminded her that she wanted to try to figure out how to be a good wife.

Ezra had told her that he had given her phone number to some of the ladies in town, and they would be in contact with her. But she hadn't heard from anyone.

She tried to tell herself to be patient as she walked through the kitchen and out the back door. The smell of chicken wafted up, and she figured that she probably ought to forgo the last trip and start making the mashed potatoes.

She didn't know how to make real ones, but she had seen a box of the powdered ones in the pantry and planned to use that.

She had never made chicken before either, but she'd been able to pull up a video on her phone.

"I'm hungry," Eugene said as he held onto Alaska's hand and they walked the short distance across the yard to the smaller house.

There were just two bedrooms in it, a small kitchen, and a dining room-living room combo. The bathroom was upstairs.

She hadn't had a choice but to put Ezra's clothes in the room that she had moved into. It was going to be a tight squeeze, and while the idea didn't really make her nervous, she had plenty of experience with men in that regard, it was the idea of being a wife, of...doing whatever it was that wives did beyond the physical. Trying to be a good one. It was kind of like trying to be a good mother. She was just winging it.

She was deep in thought, but not so deep she wasn't watching Eugene as he climbed up the steps on his hands and knees. The way Alaska had taught him when Alaska wasn't able to help.

But as Eugene stood at the top of the steps, he hadn't gotten quite far enough away from the steps, and when he lost his balance, he fell backward down the steps.

With the basket on one hip and Alice on the other, Alaska was unable to move quickly enough to catch him or even break his fall, and he tumbled to the bottom.

It was only four steps, but he did a full backward somersault.

"Eugene!" she said before she could stop herself. Someone had told her that children respond to their parents, that they see whether they should be upset or not from how their parents react, and a lot of times, things that children would just brush off were made into a big deal because of the reaction of the parents.

She clamped her mouth closed, but set the basket down, and hurried back down the steps.

To her relief, Eugene was moving. He hadn't broken his neck at least.

Thank you, Lord.

That was an automatic reaction. She had been trying to train herself to thank God for the good things that happened. After all, she had been very quick to complain about the bad things.

Eugene had been quiet for just a moment, the way kids sometimes were before they let out a bloodcurdling scream.

That scream happened as Alaska reached the bottom.

She cradled Alice in one arm while she sat down on the ground next to Eugene and tried to scoop him in her lap.

Eugene clambered around until he had his arms gripping Alaska tightly as he screamed into her chest.

Alaska appreciated the screams; that meant he was okay. She sat on the step, holding Eugene, rocking him back and forth.

"Is everything okay, young lady?" an older woman's voice said as Eugene's screams started to die down. It had been five or ten minutes since Eugene had fallen, and Alaska hadn't been sure whether he was ever going to stop crying.

"He fell down the steps."

"Oh. That's not good."

The lady, who looked to be in her early seventies, or maybe slightly older, came over and sat down beside Alaska.

"Do you want me to take the little one so you have two hands?" she asked.

"If you don't mind." Alaska didn't know the woman, but maybe that was a good thing, since all of her friends seemed to be slightly shady. While, if the woman was someone who knew Ezra, she was probably a good person. She hated to make that generalization, but it was pretty much true. Throughout her life, she had not cultivated good friendships but had a tendency to run with the wrong crowd. She sighed.

"Sometimes it's hard when they get hurt."

"Well, yeah. That happens. But I guess I was thinking that I wish I would have spent more time trying to do what was right when I was younger. It seems like I made bad decision after bad decision, and I feel like I'm in a pit with no way out." Maybe that wasn't exactly how she would explain her life, but close.

"Today's the best day to turn that around," the woman said easily, lifting Alice from Alaska's arms and smiling at the little girl, who had cried for a bit because of her brother's screams, but was generally happy, and had recovered quickly.

"I feel like it's too late. I'm twenty-five."

"My goodness. Twenty-five? You're just a baby yet. You have plenty of time to turn your life around. Why, I didn't get right with the Lord until I was in my thirties. And trust me, I made some pretty poor decisions before that."

"I'm Alaska," Alaska said, curious as to who this woman was.

"And I am Nelda. I was the nanny to the Clybourn children, and when their parents died, I came out with them."

"I didn't know they had a nanny. That seems so...old-fashioned."

"Well, a mother's helper, or whatever you want to call me. Twelve is a lot of children to have, and God knows Eunice had sorely needed the help. Especially with the first ones, since they came so fast."

"Are you still helping?" Alaska wondered why she hadn't seen the woman before.

"I'm mostly retired now. I help watch some of the grandkids. They're not mine, but they feel like it."

"I didn't know anyone had any other kids."

"If you've met Priscilla, she has two children, but they're school-age, and that's where they are right now. They were pretty upset they were going to miss working the cattle today."

"I bet," Alaska said, without any conviction. She had been thrilled when Ezra had told her she didn't need to go out, but that she could stay inside. Cattle were scary, and she had no idea how to handle them. She could only imagine that she'd end up hurt, if she didn't burst into tears.

She didn't think of herself as a weak person, but...cows were scary.

Nelda chuckled a bit as Alaska adjusted Eugene who had mostly stopped crying. There was something soothing about Nelda's voice that infused a sense of calm into Alaska as well.

"You sound like you couldn't imagine anyone being upset that they didn't get to work cattle," Nelda said, and there was humor in her tone.

"Was it that obvious?" Alaska asked with a soft chuckle.

"If you're going to be working here on the ranch, you probably ought to get used to them. It...would not be a good look for you to be afraid of cattle while you're working on a cattle ranch."

"Actually, I'm getting married to Ezra tomorrow."

She hoped she wasn't speaking out of turn. If this woman meant a lot to Ezra, maybe he wanted to tell her himself. In Alaska's experience, men were much less picky about that than women, but she didn't know Ezra very well. If she had to guess, he would thank her for saving him the trouble of having to tell someone.

Nelda gasped. She blinked and then narrowed her eyes a bit at Alaska, as though trying to see what in the world Ezra could have seen in her that would cause him to want to marry her.

"Ezra? He's getting married? To you?" There was no insult in her voice, but there was a lot of disbelief.

"I know. I can hardly believe it either. We don't really seem like two people who would end up getting married."

"Well, I suppose now that you mention it, there's that. But... Ezra is just so solid. He never does anything on the spur of the moment. He thinks everything through." She laughed, and some of her humor had come back. "It took eight years for him to finally move to Sweet Water."

"Really?" She couldn't imagine taking eight years to make a move.

"There were some hurdles to overcome. Some difficulties with the sale in Wyoming and with permits and things they needed to get in order to make this ranch what they wanted it to be, but I think Ezra would admit that some of that time was him just being methodical."

Alaska tried to picture herself taking eight years to make a decision, and she couldn't. She didn't know anyone that methodical. Maybe, maybe she wasn't the only one with some issues coming into this marriage. For some reason, the idea that Ezra wasn't perfect actually made her feel better.

"So I guess that's what I was thinking. Ezra also has a girl, Sondra, and I thought they were engaged. It wouldn't have surprised me if they stayed engaged for the next twenty years, and Ezra never made a move. He's...like I said, very methodical."

"Ezra is engaged?" Why hadn't he told her?

"Well, I don't know all the details, but I'm guessing that Sondra probably asked him, and if he even said yes, I'd be surprised. He probably grunted, and she took it as a yes. I don't think she likes him any more than he likes her, but it suited them both to be engaged."

That didn't really make Alaska feel any better. She didn't want to be married to someone who wanted to be married to someone else.

"So if Ezra decided that he was going to marry you, and you're getting married... Did you say tomorrow?"

"That's what he said." She didn't want to go into all of the issues from her past and the fact that there were people who wished her harm.

That wasn't something she was proud of, and it felt like starting off on the wrong foot to simply introduce herself and say, "yeah, I know drug dealers."

"Wow. That is...very out of character." Nelda shook her head and then bounced Alice, who had quit crying and was now smiling and gurgling up at the older woman. "Did he mention me? Because, if you are going to be here on the ranch helping at all, I'd love to take care of your children. That is, if you trust them to other people."

Alaska almost swallowed her tongue. Did she trust her children to other people? How about she *dropped them off* with other people.

But that had not been something she wanted to do. More of a necessity. Alice had been well taken care of with Travis, but she'd asked her best friend, Lucy, to keep an eye on Eugene for her for a few weeks, and Lucy had skipped town, leaving Eugene with her father. Her father was a decent person at least, but he was too old to take care of a toddler, and he ended up calling Alaska, who hadn't been able to pick him up, and she told him to take Eugene to Travis and Ellen's house.

If there was ever a person who was miserably unfit to be a mother, it was her. And it sounded like she was miserably unfit to be Ezra's wife. How was she going to get help if she didn't admit her past?

"I'd really like to learn to be a better mother." She looked at Nelda, meeting her eyes, feeling more humble than she'd ever felt in her entire life. It wasn't easy to ask for help sometimes. Especially with something so basic as motherhood. She took a breath and added, "And I'd really like to be a better wife. I... I don't really know how to do that."

Nelda's brows had gone up at the first comment. With the second, they seemed to disappear in her hairline.

It took so long for her to say anything, Alaska started to squirm and tried to figure out how she could change the subject or back out of it. It was such a weird request. People didn't talk like that. At least not where she came from.

"I'm so impressed. I very seldom get to hear people say they want help. Usually people feel like they know everything there is to know and want to jump right into teaching other people. Or bragging, or something. I think I can see some of what Ezra sees in you."

Alaska took that as a compliment. She knew that the way she looked on the outside probably didn't scream responsible adult. Especially not to someone of Nelda's age. A lot of people might say that was judgmental, but Alaska had been around enough to know that sometimes a person really could judge someone else by the way they looked. A lot of times, she deserved the judgment. The idea of being something different, better, made her want to get started right away.

"You know, I can definitely help you with the motherhood thing. It might be a good idea for you to talk to Ezra about the wife thing."

To her surprise, Alaska could feel her cheeks heating at the delicate way Nelda had said that.

"I have two children. There are certain things about being a wife that I feel like I have under control." She didn't know if she needed to be more graphic, but something kept her from it. Maybe it was Nelda's age, or perhaps that she seemed like a gentlewoman. "The other things. I mean, I assume he needs me to do the cooking and cleaning and all that stuff, and I was hardly raised to do that. In fact, the little bit of parenting I had, and a lot of the teaching that I had in school, told me that that stuff was dumb, and that I needed to have a career in order to be satisfied with my life. But it seems like someone has to cook and clean and keep the house. And I'm guessing it's not going to be Ezra."

Nelda laughed. "I agree with you, my dear. Someone needs to do it, and the Bible gives the job of keeping the house to the woman. So, to me it's less about what Ezra wants and more about what God commands."

Alaska didn't say anything, and a sound caught her ear, making her turn her head.

"It sounds like we're going to have company."

"Oh my goodness. I forgot all about the chicken!"

She jumped up, taking three steps to the house before she remembered that Nelda held Alice.

She hurried back, poor Eugene confused as she went first one way and then another. "I'm sorry to grab her and run, but I bet my chicken is ruined."

She had a sinking feeling in her stomach. It was the first time she was cooking for everyone, and she had wanted it to turn out perfectly. It would hardly be perfect if it was burnt black.

"All right, hon. If you have to run, I can't help you today, because I have an appointment with the ladies in town. But maybe you and I can get together sometime?"

Nelda sounded so relaxed, when Alaska felt like her entire world had just imploded. But she tried to calm down and give her a rational answer.

"Yes. Please. You know where I live, and maybe we'll see each other around." She didn't want to take the time to give her her phone number, because it was too much. She needed to get out of there.

"All right. Sorry about your chicken."

She nodded, knowing that there was nothing she could do, and took Alice in her arms, grabbing a hold of Eugene's hand and hurrying as fast as she could back to the larger farmhouse.

As soon as she opened the door, smoke boiled out of the kitchen, and there was no doubt that the chicken was not only burnt to a crisp, but from the glow from the oven, it was actually on fire.

Talk about a disaster. She looked at the clock as she ran to the oven. Exactly twelve noon. People would be pouring into the house at any point, and they would expect to find food. Edible food.

She absolutely hated that she was going to be a miserable failure the first time she met everyone on the ranch.

"Alaska?"

She turned. Nelda stood just inside the door, her hands on her hips.

"Yes?" She made sure she kept all impatience out of her voice. She didn't want Nelda to feel like she was brushing her off, even though she felt panic welling inside of her.

"I saw the smoke coming out the door. Give me the kids. I'll stay home from my meeting. I would say whatever you're planning to eat is ruined, but I have bacon. We can have bacon, lettuce, and tomato sandwiches, and I know that everyone will be happy with those."

Alaksa considered herself a strong woman. She'd been through an awful lot in her young life, and while she'd been knocked down a lot, she always got back up.

With her newfound faith in Christ, she expected to be able to be even stronger.

But Nelda's words made her want to cry. She swallowed through a tight throat and said, "Really?"

Maybe it was the tone of her voice, or maybe it was the relief on her face, but it made Nelda smile. "Really. Come on. We don't have much time."

59

Chapter Nine

"All right, we'll send these cows to the sale barn the day after tomorrow."

Ezra stood, looking at the half dozen or so cull cows they'd pulled from the herd during the herd check. Four of them were open, and two of them had raised such a scrawny calf, mostly because of feet issues that kept them from grazing and getting as much food as they needed, that they'd decided to send them down the road.

It was not Ezra's favorite thing, but it was something that needed to be done. They couldn't keep every cow until she died of old age, or the ranch would not be profitable.

"I have the notes, and I'll get everything typed into the computer and send a report to everyone later today," Tobias said as he held the notebook and pen in his hand.

Some people put their information in an iPad as they were doing the check, but Ezra had found that it was safer to just use a notebook. Twice, they had whatever piece of electronics they were working with ruined when a cow got out unexpectedly. Once they had to work in the rain, and they'd ended up switching to a notebook anyway, to keep their computer from getting wet.

"I'm starving. Are you guys done chewing the fat, so we can go chew actual fat?"

"I'm not sure we're having anything with fat in it. Alaska might have had chicken in the oven," Ezra said absentmindedly as he looked over at the pen of weaners, who were bawling for their moms. There were some nice calves in there, and he had high hopes for them. He just wished the price was up.

"I don't care. But I'm pretty sure I smell bacon, and I'm not going to let you talk me out of that."

"All right. Let's go in and see what she's got, because we have to move these calves if we want to get to Richard's place before dark."

Richard owned the feedlot where they'd decided to take them. But they weren't going to leave without eating.

Ezra pushed back away from the fence and started walking toward the house with Tobias and Caleb and Asher. Phoebe and Priscilla had gone to the barn to put the leftover vaccines and wormer away, and Ada, their younger sister, had gone with them. There were a few siblings who weren't currently on the ranch, so there would only be seven for lunch. Ezra hadn't given it a thought until just that moment, but he hoped that wasn't too intimidating for Alaska. He supposed someone who wasn't used to cooking for anyone might be a little intimidated cooking for seven people all of a sudden.

"Have you talked to Nelda lately?" Caleb asked as he shoved his hands in his pockets and walked like a hungry man toward the house.

Ezra bit back a smile. Caleb always did think about food first. "No. Why?"

"I just thought that if Alaska needed any help, Nelda would probably give it to her."

"She's retired. I know she still helps with the kids some, and she considers them her grandchildren, but I wouldn't ask her to take on full-time responsibility."

"Maybe she wants to," Asher murmured from his other side.

"Do you think?" He hadn't considered that. He just assumed that Nelda would enjoy her retirement. She certainly earned it after helping their mom raise twelve children.

"She always seemed like she really loved kids," Tobias said, in that thoughtful way he had. Of all his brothers, Tobias was most like him, but Ezra liked to think that he was a little bit happier, less moody, than Tobias usually was. Not that he could blame Tobias. There were some things in his past that it would be difficult for anyone to get over.

"Hey, wait up," Ada said, coming up beside them. "You guys were planning on going in there and eating everything before we got a chance."

"Survival of the fittest. Isn't that what they teach in school nowadays?" Caleb said with a grin.

"Just because they teach that in school doesn't mean we have to live it," Ada said with an eye roll.

Ezra sniffed the air, and a sense of foreboding overtook him. It smelled like something was burned. Not like burned a little, but like charred. On fire and burned to a complete crisp.

Burned flesh.

Everyone was going to give him a hard time if not only did Alaska represent danger to the family, but she also couldn't cook. And not just couldn't cook, but couldn't cook to the point where she burned the food beyond recognition. Ezra had done that himself a few times, and he recognized the smell immediately.

It had never been his job to cook for a hungry crew after they'd worked all morning, and he supposed there was a certain amount of pressure that would put on a person. Maybe Alaska didn't realize that, or maybe she tried too hard. Whatever it was, he found his step slowing and his hand feeling heavy as he reached for the door handle.

"Man. Something stinks. I sure hope it's not lunch," Caleb said with a dark look, very foreign for his face, as he stepped up on the porch.

"Whatever it is, you better not give her a hard time. It's her first time, and she's not used to this." Ezra's voice came out as commanding as it always had, even though he quaked a bit inside.

"Really? You gonna ram her down our throats and give us a hard time if we complain because her food is burnt black?" Asher said, and he didn't try to sugarcoat the fact that he wasn't very happy once the door had been opened and the smell had hit them all full force.

"Just pretend it's you. If you're capable of doing that." Ezra didn't mean to be so harsh on his brother. But Asher had to understand that he was going to marry Alaska, she was going to be part of their family, and that was the end of it.

The siblings filed in as he held the door. They stood in line silently at the sink as each one of them washed their hands, no one commenting again on the smell. But the jovial nature that had settled on their group after the work had been successfully completed had lifted, and a fog of foreboding took its place.

They piled into the kitchen, with Ezra washing his hands last and coming in after everyone else.

"You guys don't look like you're tired enough to have worked all morning. Maybe you need to get back out there and do some more work," Nelda said from where she was breaking lettuce up into a bowl.

"I take it you've met Alaska," Ezra commented, unsure whether he should be happy or upset. He didn't want Alaska to have put Nelda to work, but it would be more like Nelda to want to help. And he couldn't fault her for that. In fact, he appreciated it.

"I sure have. And we had quite the morning together, haven't we?" Nelda said with a smile at Alaska.

Alaska had her lip pulled in and bit down on it the way she did when she was unsure. The sight made something stir in Ezra's chest, and he wanted to walk over to her, touch her somehow, and...comfort her? He wasn't sure. But he had to deliberately keep his feet from turning in her direction.

"We're doing BLTs. I hope that's okay."

He nodded. "That's fine." He wasn't sure where the burnt smell came from. Maybe they'd burned a pan of bacon. He'd done that before. But he didn't ask. No one else asked about it either.

Lunch was rather subdued, with Alaska jumping up as soon as she saw that someone needed a refill in their glass, or to flip the bacon that she left in the frying pan, or to grab another jar of mayonnaise.

By the time everyone was done eating, her sandwich sat on her plate with only two bites taken out of it.

Ezra waited for his siblings to thank Alaska for the meal and then file out to the work that they had to do that afternoon before he pushed back away from the table and helped Alaska and Nelda clear off the table.

Eugene had sat at the table, eating with everyone else, and he now sat on the floor, playing with blocks.

Alice sat in her car seat, and when Ezra got up, he realized she'd fallen asleep.

"You did a good job on dinner," he said casually as he carried the plates to the kitchen.

"Thanks." She cast a glance at Nelda, who smiled encouragingly at her. There seemed to be some kind of conversation going on between the two of them before Alaska turned back to him. "I burned the chicken. It was...inedible."

"I wondered what that smell was. I thought maybe you burned a pan of bacon."

"No. The chicken was actually on fire in the oven. It was bad." She took a breath. "I'm sorry."

"It happens to everyone. You don't have to apologize. I take it Nelda must have helped you pivot pretty fast."

"Yeah. I probably would have been in a puddle on the floor crying if Nelda hadn't come up with the idea of doing BLTs. She had bacon."

"Always good to have a plan B. Especially if it includes bacon," Nelda said with her brows lifted. "If you don't mind, I'm going to see if Eugene wants to take a walk with me. We'll go see the pigs."

"You have pigs?" Eugene asked from where he'd been sitting on the floor. He jumped up and ran over, an eager look on his face.

"We sure do. Did anyone ever tell you pigs bite?"

Some of the eagerness faded from his face. "They bite?"

"They sure do. But we have a couple friendly ones who like to get scratched behind the ears. Just be careful with them. You want to come with me, and I can show you how?"

Nelda made it sound so appealing that the little boy was nodding his head before she was even done asking, and he grabbed her hand immediately when she held it out.

The door closed behind them, and Ezra found himself alone in the kitchen with the woman he was supposed to marry the next day.

She had a little smile on her face as she watched her son leave the room. He admired that but realized he had nothing in his head to say, and as her smile faded and she turned back toward him, the silence between them became awkward. He cleared his throat. All he could think of to say was to thank her for the meal, but he'd already done that.

"Nelda said you were engaged. I don't want to come between you and—"

"You're not. She decided we were getting married and forgot that I probably should consent as well. That's really all there is to it."

There might have been a little bit more, but not much.

"How old are you?" That was not the question he wanted to ask, not that it mattered. But the words were out, and he found that he was curious.

"Twenty-five. Does that matter?" She had her lip between her teeth again.

"No."

"How old are you?" she asked, and the words sounded like she was forcing them to be bold. He smiled a little at the thought.

"Thirty-eight. Is that too old?" He hadn't meant to ask that last question. He hadn't even considered that he might be. In his mind, thirty-eight wasn't nearly as old as he used to think it was, back when he was twenty-five.

She didn't answer right away, and he waited, realizing that her answer meant more to him than what he expected it to. It was important to him that she think that he would make a good husband. That he wasn't too old. She was younger than most of his siblings. In fact, just three of his siblings were her age or less.

He hadn't realized there was such an age gap. When he'd insisted that she marry him, he hadn't been thinking about anything like that.

"I wasn't expecting you to be that old. You don't look it."

"It's not too late for you to change your mind." He really didn't want to remind her of that, but he felt like he should. After all, he didn't want her to end up married to him and regret it, decide she didn't want him, and leave.

"If you've changed your mind, you can say so. You don't have to try to hope that I've changed mine."

"I wasn't hoping."

"It sounded like you were," she said, her eyes skittering over to where the car seat sat on the small table in the kitchen.

"No. I made up my mind, and I'm not going to change it, but I understand if you do. After all, if you have doubts, I'd rather you change it now than after we're married."

"I'm not going to change my mind. You've offered me something that I wasn't expecting, and I know it's better than anything else I could have hoped for. I... I just want to make sure that you don't regret it." She pulled one lip back and looked down. "I almost bumbled lunch in a major way. If it hadn't been for Nelda, I really wouldn't have had anything ready. So, maybe you should keep that in mind. I'm not trying to talk you out of anything, I'm just letting you know, I...might not be what you're hoping I am."

"It's fine. And I wouldn't feel any different if you had a big spread on the table or whether the burned chicken was all we came in to. It's just food. One meal. It doesn't say anything about a person's character for a lifetime. In fact, I think how you recover from that says a lot more about your character than messing it up in the first place. Anyone can make a mistake. But it takes someone with character to bounce back from that catastrophe and turn it into something better. You did that today."

His words made her look up, first in surprise, and then a little smile touched her lips.

She was beautiful when she smiled. The thought went through his head, but he didn't allow it to come out his mouth. He didn't want to muddy up their relationship with ideas of beauty and...love. Not the worldly kind anyway. He was marrying her to protect her. Because that was the kind of man he was. Someone who saw someone who needed help, and he would help them however he could, even if it meant committing to them for a lifetime. Her babies needed a father, and Alaska needed a break. Marrying him would solve both of those problems. That was all there was to it. Any kind of emotional entanglement would just complicate things.

"Nelda is going to help me with the kids. I don't really know how to be a mom," she said, looking at him underneath her brows.

"Nelda is really good. I should have talked to her before this. I don't know what her thoughts are, but if she's willing to help you, you couldn't have anyone better."

"But when I asked her about being a good wife, she told me I needed to talk to you."

He didn't really understand what she was saying about being a good wife. He supposed there were things that she could do that would irritate him, and they would figure those things out.

"I think we talked about there being a group of ladies that you could talk to. I sent a text to Bernadine, who kind of spearheads things. She said she would drop by or call you. Hasn't she?"

"No."

"It's been less than a day. Let's give her a little more time before I nudge her again, okay?"

She nodded. "So you don't want to tell me what you want me to do as your wife?"

He started to turn, thinking the conversation was over, but her words made him stop and just stare at the floor.

"Can you give me a little time to think about it? I... I'm not sure what you're asking. Sometimes I think that maybe you just have to step into something before you figure out the things that don't work. Does that make sense?"

"Yeah. I guess. I guess... I want to have a list. I want to know exactly what I have to do in order to, I don't know, win? Something like that."

"Just be faithful. Just be faithful, and give me grace when I'm not the husband you think I should be." That seemed to be a new idea for her. Because she tilted her head to the side, and there was a line between her brows.

"Give you grace?"

"Sometimes when you mess up, you need someone to say, it's okay. And not get mad, and give you the silent treatment for six days, and make you grovel on your hands and knees for a year before forgiveness is extended. Grace is...giving someone something they don't deserve. Special favor. So, if you had served burnt chicken for lunch, and I had tried to eat it anyway, and I hadn't gotten upset, and I had thanked you for the meal, and we had gone on as though it hadn't been a bad thing, I think that would qualify as giving grace." He grinned. "Maybe you should have done that, just to see if maybe I need to grow in grace. After all, I was pretty hungry when I walked in, and I might've been a little short tempered. I think giving grace is just something that we need to practice and get better at. Actually, there might be a lot of things that we need to practice and get better at."

Unbidden, an idea popped in his mind that he tried to push aside. But it lingered. He hadn't kissed many women in his life at all. He'd been more focused on making a living and then raising his siblings after his parents had died. Having Sondra as a girlfriend took a lot of pressure off, and he realized that he reached the ripe old age of thirty-eight, and maybe he needed some practice in the physical side of marriage. He might not be any good. The idea hadn't really crossed his mind before that, but now that he had someone standing in front of him, asking him how to be a good wife, it made him think that maybe he was going to need to learn how to be a good husband. And not just a good provider.

"I might need grace in a few areas," he murmured.

She shook her head like she didn't believe him, and he didn't want to elaborate. There was plenty of time to find out. Although, in his mind's eye, he could almost hear his dad saying, *some things just come naturally, son*. He wondered if that was one of those things.

"Well, I better get back out. I'll have more time to talk in the evenings, usually. Typically, we don't spend too much time on dinner."

"That's fine. I am... I have lots of things to do anyway."

"Are you okay?" he asked, not knowing exactly what she might need but figuring that it was his job to try to make sure that her needs were taken care of.

"I'm fine. I've got most of your stuff moved over to the house, and I'll just keep working on that." She paused. "Have you heard anything from the police?"

"No. I haven't. But I can call one of my buddies who's on the force and whom I know a little bit. Do you want me to ask?"

"No."

"Are you afraid?" He hadn't really given it too much thought once they started working cows. He considered that morning that they might have visitors, but the thought had slid away without too much concern on his part. But he wasn't the one who had been traumatized yesterday.

"No. I... I feel like you mean it when you say you're going to protect me."

"I mean it as much as I can."

She nodded. "I guess that's all I can ask for."

She hadn't even really asked for that. He volunteered for it.

It felt like there was something missing. Something he should do. Something that should alleviate the rest of the awkwardness that had fallen between them, but he couldn't think of what it was, so he just jerked his head, while she looked away, and he strode out of the house. Surely over time, things would feel more natural between them. He hoped so.

Chapter Ten

Today was her wedding day.

Alaska stretched and rolled over, looking out the window. The sun was well up in the sky, and she was pretty sure that everyone would have eaten breakfast and be out working for the day.

She managed to talk to Claudia for just a couple minutes the night before and had offered to cook breakfast or lunch or supper or something. She wanted to be able to do something on the farm. Be a help. Claudia had smiled and said that it was no problem, she loved cooking and that Alaska didn't need to concern herself with it.

Alaska knew that Claudia was just being kind, and she didn't understand that Alaska needed a job. She'd been hired to be Ezra's personal assistant, but all the family pitched in with everything. She needed to feel...like she wasn't just a leech hanging out here, taking from everybody.

That was a terrible way to explain it, but it was how she felt.

Alice had been up twice in the middle of the night, and while Alaska appreciated the fact that she hadn't had to get up early and cook breakfast for everyone, she still would prefer to have a job.

She felt...a little lost.

"Hello? Is anyone home?" A voice drifted upstairs, and Alaska jumped out of bed.

"I'm here! I'll be down in a second," she added, grabbing the clothes that she laid out the night before and putting them on as quickly as she could. A couple of minutes later, she hurried down the steps.

"I'm sorry. I was just lying in bed thinking that there really wasn't any reason to get up."

She thought that sounded a little sad and wished she could take it back and rephrase it, but the words were out there.

"I'm Bernadine, and Ezra told me that you and I might have some things to talk about." Bernadine smiled, completely at home in what Alaska assumed was a strange house. She was an older lady, maybe in her seventies, the same as Nelda, and she seemed spry and energetic. "I brought some groceries, because today I was planning on making a meal for my friend Agathe. I thought you could help me with it."

"I'd love to," Alaska said immediately. "But I might have to quit and take care of my children. Neither one of them are awake right now."

Normally Eugene didn't sleep as long as he had already that morning, but Alaska had to admit that it had been a few months since she had taken care of Eugene on a regular basis. The thought made her sad, and she had to turn her mind away from that. She had decided to go down a different trail, and she would not look back.

"I heard you had two little ones. A baby and a toddler?"

"That's right. A little girl, Alice, and Eugene is two."

"Wow. You have your hands full. Those ages are fun, but they're a lot of work too." While there was compassion in Bernadine's voice, she was also a very no-nonsense type of lady, as she walked through the living room and into the kitchen, setting two bags of groceries on the counter.

"Yeah." Alaska realized she felt a little overwhelmed. Bernadine was like a force of nature.

"All right. I have everything we need to make my delicious spinach and sun-dried tomato orzo bake. My friend Agathe is taking care of her husband who's in the early stages of Alzheimer's. I don't know what else to do for her, so I just make food."

There was some pain hidden in her words, and Alaska didn't have any trouble picking up on that immediately.

"I thought you and I can talk while we cook, and then maybe Agathe will have some time to talk to us at some point. If there's anyone who knows how to be a good wife, it's her. It's...hard right now, especially since she and Jim were always so much in love."

"I bet that would be hard." Alaska didn't want to think about the end of her life. She'd barely gotten started on the beginning. Although, that might be something she faced. She hadn't realized that Ezra was so much older than she was. He was thirty-eight. That seemed...really old.

But it didn't change the fact that she would still marry him. And she supposed, surely he thought that her age was really young.

She didn't have any time to continue that train of thought because Bernadine was talking again.

"Go ahead and get a casserole dish out. This is super easy to make. We're going to put the ingredients right in the dish."

"That sounds easy all right," Alaska said, and then she figured she might as well add, "This is my second day in this kitchen. I probably don't have any more idea of where the pans are than you do. So, I'm just going to be hunting for them. I wanted to warn you."

"Well, don't be shy. If you're going to be a good wife, you have to just jump in and start swimming. You might not know how to swim, but you're not gonna learn if you just stand around. You have to get in the water at least."

Alaska couldn't argue with that, and she went about opening drawers and doors until she found the pan.

Pulling one out, she held it up. "Will this work?"

"That's perfect," Bernadine said, setting the paper bag that she'd emptied on the chair. "We'll use that as our garbage can. Now, set that on the counter here."

She started to talk about how she was going to make the food, and she gave Alaska a package of orzo to open.

"Men are pretty simple. They want us to feed them, they want you to respect them, and they want..." Bernadine lifted her brow. "I think you're probably okay in that regard."

For the second time in two days, Alaska felt her cheeks heating. She wouldn't have thought she could get embarrassed, but she found out that she was wrong.

"It's definitely the other things I'm looking for advice on," she said quickly, trying to pretend she wasn't embarrassed. "I just never saw a good relationship. I don't know a single couple that's happy together, even if they're still together. Certainly my parents weren't a good example." She didn't even want to go there. "And I've never had a relationship that lasted very long or felt...good."

"Well, you hit the jackpot with Ezra. I really don't think you need to do too much, and he's going to treat you well anyway. But he's probably going to be a typical man too, and by that, I mean he might have to learn that you don't want advice, you just want him to commiserate."

"But I do like advice," Alaska said immediately.

"Well then, he'll probably be better at that. Sometimes men want to fix our problems instead of just listening to them."

"I'd rather have someone tell me how to fix it than just listen to me complain," Alaska said, and she meant it. She knew that there were some women who just wanted people to agree with them. That wasn't her.

"You'll have to tell him that. Maybe he's learned from his sisters that females prefer to have someone pat them on the back and make tsking sounds. I know I've had my share of men who were so hardheaded, they didn't even care. At least it felt like they didn't. You tell them how terrible your life was, and they'd be like, 'that's great, is supper ready yet?'" She rolled her eyes.

Alaska laughed. That did sound like a typical man.

"Here. I think I hear one of your little ones crying. You stir this, and I'll go get them."

Bernadine thrust the spoon at her and then proceeded to walk out of the kitchen and up the stairs.

Alaska had never met anyone who was so at home in someone else's house. She certainly wouldn't be running up the stairs to grab someone else's children, but...maybe that was the way things were done around here.

Or maybe Bernadine was just one of a kind. Maybe that was why Ezra thought she would be a good person to talk to Alaska. She had to remember that Ezra had chosen this woman himself. Whatever she had to say, Alaska wanted to listen.

"Look who I found," Bernadine said, a few minutes later, as she came back downstairs with Eugene on her hip. She had clothes for him in her hand as well.

She gave instructions to Alaska while she changed his diaper and put his clothes on. She seemed to do everything effortlessly, when Alaska knew that she would be stumbling and bumbling around, trying to figure out what to do next.

"All right. You can put that in the oven for twenty minutes." She had finished changing Eugene, and Alaska's son was much happier than he normally was in the morning when she had him herself.

It was a little bit discouraging. But she put the orzo bake in the oven, and then Bernadine said, "Your baby was up, but she was happy, so I didn't grab her. We can go on back up and get her."

She didn't leave any room for conversation, and Alaska dutifully followed her back up the stairs.

Fifteen minutes later, they were back downstairs with two freshly changed children, and Bernadine made a bottle for Alice while directing Alaska to put some scrambled eggs in the pan for Eugene.

Was this the way she normally ran her kitchen? It felt so efficient. Alaska figured that, better than talking to her, she was just showing her how she could take things in hand. She had given the children attention, but she kept her eye out for the other things that needed to be done, giving Alaska instructions, figuring out where the bottles were, and determining what Eugene could eat for breakfast.

Sometimes it took Alaska half an hour or more just to figure out what in the world they were going to eat.

And Eugene seemed to like his eggs just fine, as she set the plate in front of him, and he began to eat eagerly.

"I wish things went this smoothly when I am alone," Alaska said.

"I've had plenty of years of experience. You learn how to do things, and then they come naturally. But you can't expect to do things perfectly the first time. Or the second time. You have to give yourself grace."

That was the second time she heard that—grace—in two days.

"Ezra talked about grace yesterday. Only... It was like not getting angry for mistakes."

"And especially mistakes that maybe you should get angry for. After all, as a mom, you expect yourself to know how to be a mom, but sometimes you don't. Sometimes you mess up. Sometimes you just have to allow yourself the space to make mistakes, accept them, and then move on. Of course, we always try to do better, but we don't sit around and bemoan the fact that we messed something up."

"But people might get mad at us," Alaska said. That had been something she struggled with a lot. She hated it when people got upset with her. Maybe that was part of the reason it had taken her so long to get out of the world of drugs and alcohol and promiscuity. Sure, change was hard, but she knew it was going to make people mad at her. Case in point was the police at her house, yesterday.

"You can't worry about that. Now, I'm not saying that you should be deliberately unkind to people. Of course you shouldn't. But you cannot allow the idea that someone might be upset with you to ruin your life. You have to put your eyes on Jesus. And then, whatever you do, you know it's the right thing. If you're living to please Him, to serve Him, to do what He wants, then you might upset some people. And that's just the way life goes."

"But doesn't Jesus want us to love everyone? Doesn't that mean that we won't deliberately make anyone mad?"

"The key word there is deliberately. If you make a mistake, apologize and move on. You don't need to sit around and bite your nails, thinking and overthinking about how you should have done things differently. Do you know how much time you waste doing that?"

Alaska didn't have a chance to answer.

"You only have one life. Do you really want to spend your life sitting around thinking about all the things that you wish you could change? That's a waste. Especially if they're tiny little things, a minor accident. Now, there is a place and a time for you to think about the things that you've done wrong and the things you want to change in the future, but getting all upset and worrying over stuff is a waste of time."

"I think I understand."

"Eugene, look at you. You ate all of your egg. What a good boy."

Bernadine walked over to the tray and handed Eugene a cracker. Alaska hadn't even seen her get it. "All right. We need to pull that out of the oven, stir it, and we're going to add some spinach and cheese, and bake it just a little bit more."

Alaska grabbed a pot holder and got the casserole dish out of the oven as Bernadine had instructed. Under her guidance, she added the last ingredients and put it back in the oven.

"Do you think I'll ever be as organized as what you are?" Alaska said as she straightened. How was she going to do it all? Take care of the kids, cook, clean, do laundry, help on the farm, and be a good wife? It seemed overwhelming. She couldn't imagine trying to have a full-time job and do all of the things.

"Yes. I do. It will come slowly, gradually, until one day you realize that things that used to be hard aren't anymore. It's kind of like if you've ever trained for any kind of sports. Or... If you practice the piano or an instrument. You just slowly get better. Until one day, you look back on the things you've done, and it shocks you that you're so much farther on than what you used to be."

"I guess I'll take your word for it."

"A year from now, we'll talk." Bernadine smiled. "Actually, I hope we talk a good bit between now and then. But we'll look back then. Assess where you were and where you're at now."

"I try not to look back." Alaska felt like she needed to be honest.

"And I think that's generally a good idea. We can't go back, so what's the point in looking back and wishing we were back there. But God commanded the Israelites to keep feast days so that they would remember His goodness, and His mercy, and the way He brought them out of Egypt. So, I definitely think looking back, and celebrating your victories, is something that God wants us to do. Especially when we're looking at what God has done. Which, as impossible as everything looks sometimes, you know you can't do it without Him."

Alaska hadn't considered that. God would help her. He could make the impossible possible. And that was why she didn't have to worry about whether or not she'd ever learn everything. She didn't have to worry about it. God would make sure it happened. Although, she assumed that God expected her to work as hard as she could. It wasn't like He was just going to drop victories in her lap without her having to fight for them.

"Knock, knock!"

Alaska turned with surprise as Nelda walked into the kitchen.

"Good morning!" she said, her cheeks red, her eyes shining. She wore bright white sneakers with black leggings and a form-fitting T-shirt. She looked athletic and fit and like she had far more energy than Alaska could even dream of having.

Chapter Eleven

"Good morning," Alaska and Bernadine both said.

"How's the new bride on her wedding day?" Nelda asked, going over to the high chair and dropping a kiss on the top of Eugene's head. Eugene tried to reach for her with his hands as cracker crumbs fell to the floor.

Alaska had not forgotten it was her wedding day, but she hadn't really been dwelling on it either. Ezra had said that he wanted to go after the noon meal because he wanted to get some work done first. Since he wasn't even taking a full day off work, she figured that she ought not to make such a big deal about it, even though part of her wanted to. It wasn't every day that a person got married. Of course, she had some major regrets about the way she treated someone's marriage, and...she wasn't sure what to do about it.

"I guess I'm fine."

"You guess?" Nelda asked, straightening up and running one finger down Eugene's pudgy cheek.

"Sure. I mean, Ezra isn't really making a big deal about it, so I haven't been thinking about it too much either."

"Well, you should probably make sure that it's what you want to do. This is something that should be irreversible."

"Right." Divorce came all too easily for some people, but she didn't want that to be something that she did. Of course, her track record wasn't exactly great. And she couldn't fix it, but she could... She had to talk to Ezra when he got in. There was something she definitely needed to do before they got married.

She couldn't believe she hadn't thought about it before this.

"We were hoping that it would be okay with you if Nelda took the children so that you and I could go and see Agathe together, without them."

"Are you sure you don't mind?" She turned to Nelda, surprised. She wasn't used to not doing things with her children. That was part of the reason she'd given them to other people. Because having them with her made everything she did so much harder. And of course, trying to have a job and pay someone to watch her kids typically didn't leave much money left over at all. It was almost impossible to get ahead while paying for child care.

"I don't mind at all. I got up this morning with eager anticipation, because I thought I was going to get to spend the day with two cuties," Nelda said, coming over and taking Alice into her arms. Alice was done with the bottle, and Nelda grabbed a tea towel, throwing it over her shoulder and putting the baby up, patting her back to burp her like an expert. If she had helped to raise twelve children, she would definitely be considered an expert in Alaska's view.

"Well then, it's okay with me. Thank you." She couldn't help but be surprised. She wasn't used to people just coming in and volunteering to help her. The first that she had any idea that people could be so kind was with Travis and Ellen. They had accepted Alice and taken as good care of her as though she were their own child. Unlike Lucy, whom she'd given Eugene to and who had dropped him off with her dad and skipped town. And Lucy had been someone she had considered a friend.

"What's the matter?" Bernadine said, bending over and trying to look in her eyes.

"I guess I'm just not used to people being nice to me," she said, being as honest as she could.

"Oh, honey." Bernadine took two steps and wrapped her arms around her. The feeling made Alaska want to cry. She wasn't used to someone caring about her, wondering what was wrong, or wanting to hug her. She couldn't remember any feeling of safety and warmth in her mother's arms, and this felt even better.

She wrapped her arms around Bernadine and hugged her back, blinking back the tears that wanted to fall. She couldn't help the past, but she could try to make something better of the future. Not just for herself, but for her children too.

"That's what we're here for. All of us, to support other people. I think we get really confused and think we're just here for ourselves. We start to live for ourselves, care only about ourselves, and forget that's not what the purpose of life is."

"I've often wondered what the purpose of life was." Alaska's words were soft. She laid awake at night often, wondering what in the world she was living for. Sometimes things just felt so hopeless. And it didn't seem like it was worth it to get up in the morning and keep striving, for what?

Then, after she turned her life over to Christ, she understood that she was supposed to be living for Jesus, but she still didn't really understand what that meant.

"The Bible says that we're here to glorify God and live to serve Him. If you look at Jesus's life on earth, most of his life was about others and living for them. I think sometimes we get our focus on others rather than ourselves, and then we have an idea about life and its purpose. Because when we work to help others, then we have a reason for living."

"Children give us a purpose. And that's living for others. They demand so much of us, it's almost impossible to live for yourself when you have babies around." Bernadine went back to the stove and took the orzo bake out. It smelled so good. "I think we ought to try to take this while it's hot. Are you ready to go?"

Alaska said, "Sure."

"And I've got the kids. We'll finish eating, and then I'll probably take them to my place. It's not far, just down the road a piece, behind the barn."

"It didn't even occur to me to wonder where you lived. There are so many people coming and going, and I haven't even gotten familiar with all the buildings on the ranch."

"It's a big place, that's for sure."

Alaska nodded. She would have to take Nelda's word for it since she hadn't really seen much at all.

She and Bernadine left shortly after, with her holding the hot casserole dish on her lap in a carrying case.

"It's not far to Agathe's," Bernadine said as she pulled the car down the driveway.

Alaska listened to her, but she looked off to the horizon where there were two four-wheelers moving down what looked like a road heading out toward one of the fields. She thought it was Ezra on the first one, but she couldn't be sure. It was funny how she wanted to just get a glimpse of him. Like she somehow needed to see him. Or at least had a deep desire to.

"I was so nervous on my wedding day. You seem pretty calm." Maybe Bernadine was just trying to make conversation, but it made Alaska feel like there was something wrong with her.

"I guess I've done some things in my life that I really regret. Looking back, I made a lot of stupid choices. Marrying Ezra doesn't seem like it is even close to fitting in the category of any of my other dumb ideas."

"You two seem so very different. But sometimes people who are different are compatible. The thing is, you just have to learn to share some common interests and maybe even learn to know each other a little." She paused for a moment. "I don't know Ezra that well, but he seems like he might be a hard man to get to know. And you have to remember that you can't change him. He might not want to get to know you, he might not be interested, and he might not be interested in doing things that you enjoy. If you're getting married to him, you can't depend on equal sharing of fifty-fifty or a hundred or whatever you hear counselors say. If you want to make sure that your marriage lasts, you have to put everything you can into it and not worry about what he does."

"That doesn't seem very fair," Alaska pointed out.

"I don't think you see anything about things being fair in the Bible. God is the righteous judge. And then He gives us commands, and He wants us to follow them and let Him worry about what's fair and what's not fair." She put a turn signal on and pulled into a driveway.

"Sometimes we just have to have faith that everything's going to work out, and when we get to heaven, we'll see all of the unfairness washed away, and things will seem right to us. I don't know how else to explain it. But if you're looking for a marriage that's entirely fair, I don't think you're going to find one."

Alaska had been looking for advice on her marriage, but that wasn't exactly the kind of advice she wanted to hear. She wanted to hear that both of them were responsible for their marriage, and that Ezra had to pull as much weight as she did, and that it wasn't all going to be on her shoulders.

If she were married to a good man, and she considered that Ezra was most likely a good man, it would not be on her shoulders. But if it weren't, she understood that Bernadine was saying that if she wanted to keep her vows, she was going to have to be the one to make the effort and not depend on anyone else. The thought was sobering.

"Now, Agathe's husband Jim sometimes knows who people are, and sometimes he doesn't. I'm just warning you."

"All right," Alaska said. She hadn't been around too many people with Alzheimer's, but she understood that it took their memories. It seemed sad. Especially for Agathe.

They got out of the car, with Alaska being very careful to not spill the casserole. It seemed silly to put all the work into doing a good deed for someone and then mess it up just steps from her house.

It was a cute little bungalow, with light blue siding, and a little walk that would probably have flowers beside it if it were later in the season, or maybe if Agathe had more time on her hands.

There were neighbors on each side, although there was a nice-sized yard, and the house was set back from the road just a little.

It looked like a quaint and friendly place to live. So suburban and middle class that it made Alaska's heart hurt. This was the kind of house that she had always looked at from the outside but had never set foot in. Now all of a sudden, with Ezra's protection, she was doing things she never thought she would.

It didn't really occur to her to look around and make sure that she was safe. But as she stepped up the sidewalk, she suddenly wondered if perhaps her presence here would be endangering the people in this house. She hadn't considered that at all. Being on the ranch wasn't something she worried about. Ezra said they would protect her, and it was less about her bringing people on them and more about him watching out for her. Although Ezra had not said that she shouldn't leave the ranch, now she wondered if maybe she shouldn't have.

And on the heels of that thought came another one. She left her children there alone.

Nelda was in great physical shape, but she was still a senior citizen and too sweet and kind to think ill of anyone. If someone came to take her children, Alaska wouldn't want Nelda to get hurt any more than she wanted her children to suffer.

The thought scared her enough that Bernadine looked at her after she knocked on the door. "Are you okay?" she asked.

"I'm fine."

"Your face is kind of white, and you went real silent there."

"I guess I'm not used to visiting people. This isn't something I normally do."

"Don't worry. We're not going to stay long. Agathe has her hands full, and you have a wedding." Bernadine smiled like it was exciting.

Alaska supposed she was looking forward to getting married, but more because it would solve some problems for her than because of the typical reasons a bride might look forward to her wedding.

Although, spending the rest of her life with Ezra did not present a hardship in her eyes.

"Bernadine! Come on in." The lady who arrived at the door opened it wide, smiling like she took great pleasure in having visitors.

"We'll come in, but we're not staying. We just wanted to deliver a little casserole for you, to try to take the burden off a little bit."

"That's so thoughtful of you," she said as they walked in. "Jim is having a good day today," she said in a low voice.

Bernadine nodded and bent forward just a bit, her voice pitched so low that Alaska had trouble hearing. "It's good hearing that. I know it makes it easier on you."

Agathe smiled and nodded.

Bernadine straightened and turned to Alaska. "This is Alaska, she's going to be out at the ranch, and she's marrying Ezra."

"Oh. Ezra is quite a catch. I love the tall, dark, and silent types." Agathe smiled a little bit of a dreamy smile. "That's what caught my eye with Jim. I know his hair is white now, and he's a little stooped from age, but back in the day, he was quite the dashing soldier, and he stole this country girl's heart so easily."

Her voice, with a slight French accent, was melodic and dulcet, and she seemed so friendly and sweet that Alaska had to smile as she carefully took the proffered hand and shook it.

"Ezra definitely is a man of character, and I'm so honored that he's going to marry me."

She couldn't really say that they were madly in love with each other or act like it was a love match. That would be lying. So she didn't.

Even though she kind of wished she could.

"We have company. That's nice. And it looks like they brought food. That's the best kind." A tall, slightly stooped man, with bright white hair, walked into the room.

"Jim, this is Bernadine, my friend from our aquatics group, and Alaska. She is from the Sweet View Ranch, and she'll be marrying the oldest brother there, Ezra."

"Alaska. That's a great state. Have you ever been there?" Jim said, coming forward with his hand out.

Alaska could see how someone as refined and sweet as Agathe would have been charmed by him. There were definitely signs of the dashing and charming man he used to be. Alaska found herself grinning like a girl as she shook his hand.

"No. I've never been there, but I'd like to go sometime." There were tons of things she'd love to do. Places she'd like to see, but as a mom of two small children and someone who was getting married to a man who was a dedicated rancher, she knew that her life probably wouldn't be one of travel to exotic locations.

"You won't regret it. It's beautiful."

Jim stepped back and put his arm around Agathe. Obviously, they were still in love after all of the years that had gone by. She could picture them as a young couple, smiling and laughing at each other, seeking a place to be alone together. They seemed like the kind of couple that were happier by themselves. They would never run out of things to talk about and always be interested in making sure that the other one was happy. Both of them seemed like really great people. As Bernadine talked for just a bit before excusing them so they could leave, Alaska wondered if that was how she and Ezra would look after years together. She hoped so.

Chapter Twelve

"This is really good. Did you make it?" Jim asked as they sat eating the spinach and sun-dried tomato orzo bake that Bernadine and Alaska brought just that morning.

"It is delicious. And no, my friends Bernadine and Alaska brought it this morning."

"Are you sure? I don't really remember you making anything like this before, but I don't know this Bernadine you're talking about. And Alaska? Isn't that a state?"

She hated it when his memory faded in and out. Well, she hated it when his memory went out. It made her feel so...ungrounded. Jim had always been a rock. The person that she depended on. They hardly ever went anywhere without the other one, and her whole life centered around him. Especially after he retired. They'd done so many fun things together, and she couldn't imagine having a better life partner.

Now, when she really needed him, as she was growing older herself, he was leaving her, and he didn't even know it.

"I'm sure. But I can get the recipe and I can make it. If you like it."

"Yeah. Do you know how to cook?"

She tried to fight back tears. He used to tease her that she was French so she was an excellent cook, even though when they got married, she really wasn't. She had learned, because back when she was married, that was what a good wife did. Now, women weren't expected to know how to cook. She was glad she'd grown up in a different age. Cooking had given her a lot of satisfaction. Even if it wasn't the traditional French meals that her mother had made growing up. She'd learned to cook like an American.

"I've cooked for you for years."

"You have?" Jim set his fork on his plate and peered over his glasses at her. "Do I know you?"

She never knew what to say when he asked that question. Obviously he didn't remember knowing her, and when she said yes, it just confused him more and even upset him, because he couldn't remember. But if she said no, then he would ask what she was doing in his house. Or, worse, he'd ask where his house was and get up and start off like he was going to go find it.

Jim had never been violent, and he had never been a man who was prone to fits of temper, and she had never been scared.

But lately, he'd been very insistent on his way.

"You do know me. We've known each other for years. I think sometimes we just forget as we grow older."

"Oh. Do you think I would forget someone as pretty as you?"

"Well, I hope not. But if you have, I guess we could have some fun getting reacquainted." She said her words lightly and gave him a little, teasing smile, the flirty kind of smile she'd given him all throughout their marriage. Except, she'd never had to reintroduce herself to him.

Sometimes when she got her hair styled in a different type of way, he would tease her about going to bed with a new woman, and she would tease him back. It was kind of fun to play little pretend games like that. It kept their marriage fresh and exciting, and she enjoyed it.

Except now, with him not knowing her, it was all too serious and it scared her. Her life was changing. The rock she'd always depended on was suddenly not as solid as she thought it was, and she had to turn more and more to the Lord for strength and support.

Maybe she'd depended more on Jim than she had on the Lord throughout her life. That was one of the things that she learned in the time she'd been dealing with her husband and his Alzheimer's. She always said that God was the most important thing in her life, but she found out that maybe that wasn't quite as true as she wanted it to be.

"Maybe we can do that after my nap. I'm getting tired. I do take a nap after lunch, don't I?" Jim's brows furrowed, and he looked at her as though she were his caretaker or his mother, instead of his wife.

"Sometimes," she said, being honest. He didn't typically take a nap, but as they got older, naps had been something that had become a little bit more common.

He pushed back away from the table and looked at her. "Do we know each other well enough to take a nap together?" His brows were puzzled, as though he were trying to figure out what their relationship actually was.

"I think we do. We've been married for more than fifty years. I'm pretty sure it's okay for us to sleep together."

"Well, in that case, I'll take the pretty girl with me." He held out his hand, and she slid hers into his, the feeling so familiar, so nostalgic, bringing back all of the memories of their years together, that she had to fight back tears.

It wasn't hard to leave the table, leave the leftovers, leave the mess for later. It was easy for her to think that there wouldn't be very many times like this left. She had to enjoy them while she could.

As she walked away, down the hall toward their bedroom, she remembered that Rhoda had left a message about an Alzheimer's group that was meeting in the Olympic training center and asked if Agathe would like to join.

When she got up, she'd have to remember to call and see what she needed to do. This was one of the hardest things, if not the hardest thing she'd ever done. She definitely could use some support for it.

Another thing she wanted to do was to make sure that she continued to develop a relationship with the Lord and make sure that He was her anchor. It was obvious that she was losing Jim, and she needed to have God to hold onto, to keep her from feeling unmoored, like her life was in flux. It was a disconcerting feeling that made her want to hang on to whatever was closest.

She had a feeling that things were going to get a lot harder before they got better.

Chapter Thirteen

"We need to get the fence fixed in the upper pasture. We have those mamas that just lost their babies there, and we need to make sure the fence is good enough to keep them in." Ezra lifted his hat and ran a hand through his hair. There were so many things to do and not enough time to do them. That's the way he always felt.

"I guess you won't be helping with that. You have to go to Rockerton." Caleb lifted a brow at him, but there were questions in his eyes. Asher had been the only brother that had truly questioned him, and that was only because he wanted to make sure his siblings were safe.

Still, if it were him, he certainly would want to say something to any of his brothers since he didn't think it was a good idea to get married after meeting a woman less than a week prior.

"Yeah. I wish I could help you, but I can't today. There will be work to do tomorrow; there always is."

Caleb snorted, and then he nodded, clasping his brother on the shoulder. "You know, I've never known you to do anything crazy. You always make the best decisions. I think this is the first time in my life I'm questioning what in the world you're thinking. Except, maybe when Sondra went around announcing that you guys were engaged. But even then, I just assumed she put words in your mouth."

"That's basically what happened." Ezra didn't really want to talk about it. Although, he supposed he should. It was only fair to his siblings. He certainly would want to talk to him about it.

But, unless he wanted to get married in the clothes he'd worked in all morning, he needed to get to the house to change. He'd told her they'd leave at one o'clock, and he and Caleb had stayed out, fixing the float on the water trough rather than going in for lunch. Now, he needed to get himself in there and get cleaned up, or she was going to think that he didn't want to marry her.

It was crazy, but thinking about Alaska made something warm tug at his heart.

"I'll get this stuff gathered up. You go on ahead," Caleb said, after a short silence, where he must have figured out that Ezra wasn't going to say anything more about Sondra and their engagement.

He really couldn't without speaking poorly of Sondra, which he didn't want to do.

He jerked his head, and then walked to his four wheeler, starting it and taking a second to allow his gaze to roam over the fields, green and lush in the spring, dotted by black cattle, and a few brown ones, a new breed that they'd introduced to try to improve the quality of their meat. He hadn't been afraid to take risks, to take chances, and to try to always improve.

As he drove along the road that led toward the buildings, he could look across and see a white car coming down the driveway.

He had to do a double take because it looked an awful lot like Sondra's car. But, he just talked to her yesterday, and he'd broken up with her like he planned, although it hadn't been any easier than what he thought it was going to be. He hated the conversation, that he even had to do it, and was glad that part of his life was over.

Maybe part of marrying Alaska was because he knew he wasn't good in this area of his life. He'd found someone he could just marry without trying to go through the awkwardness of getting to know her, figuring out what she liked, and wondering if she was going to break up with him.

He could just focus on work.

Even when he thought about that, he had a nagging voice in the back of his head reminding him that he couldn't expect to have a strong marriage if he didn't want to put any effort into it.

He knew it, he just...probably like any human didn't want to spend a lot of time doing something that he was uncomfortable doing, and wasn't any good at.

He squinted at the car, looking out from under the brim of his cowboy hat.

A brisk breeze, never ending in North Dakota, stirred the grass, making the shushing sound that he loved. But he didn't notice. Because, he was absolutely sure that was the exact make and model of Sondra's car.

He didn't know anyone else in Sweet Water who drove that kind and color, and he tried to think of what time it was when he had spoken with her the day before.

Would she have had time to drive all of this way?

It didn't take much thought before he realized that she absolutely could have. It was only about eight hours to where they'd lived in Wyoming.

Sondra could have made the trip easily.

Just because it was the way things usually happened, he wasn't surprised when in the distance, he could see another car turning off the main road and pulling down the drive. He almost laughed to himself. That would be Bernadine bringing Alaska home.

A couple of his brothers had come back from lunch and said that she had gone with Bernadine to take a meal to Agathe, but that she would be back in plenty of time to get married.

They teased him about it a bit, when they'd stopped in where he and Caleb were fixing the float on the water trough.

He let their teasing roll in one ear and out the other, but when he saw the car pull in, he was sure that was who it was, even though he didn't know what kind of car Bernadine drove.

He wanted to turn the four wheeler around and take off to the furthest part of the ranch.

But he didn't want to be a coward.

He had been the head of the house for a long time now. Even before his parents had passed away, his dad had put a lot of responsibility on his shoulders, not just because he had an aptitude for it, but because he didn't turn around and run when things got hard.

He squared his shoulders, lifted his chin, and said a short prayer. He didn't even know what to pray, other than *help me Lord*. This was not something he was good at, and a confrontation between the woman who thought she was engaged to him, and the one that he was supposed to marry today, was not going to be pretty.

And then he knew what to pray for. Wisdom. Compassion. And that elusive quality that enabled a person to smooth things out, to calm someone down, even when they didn't want to be calmed down. *Charm*. That's what he needed. And that's what he lacked. That's what he'd always lacked. He was conscientious, dependable, the kind of person that got things done, and responsible, but he didn't typically do it with an abundance of charm. That was Caleb, or one of his other brothers.

Lord, I feel like I might as well ask you if you could help me learn to fly. But, right now, I could really use some charm.

It wasn't that he didn't have faith that God could work miracles, because he did. He just kind of figured that God wanted him to muddle through his life with the personality that God had given him, and not always need something extra.

Regardless, he continued driving toward the house, arriving after Sondra, who had already gotten out of her car, and was not in a good mood, if the storm clouds on her face were any indication, and shortly before Bernadine pulled in beside Sondra's car, with, of course, Alaska's door right beside where Sondra stood.

Thankfully, Sondra's eyes were on him as he parked the four wheeler on the other side of her car.

It wasn't a deliberate move. He would prefer to have parked behind or between the two cars, but, part of him thought that Sondra might leave in an angry huff, and it might be better to not have anything parked behind her car that she could run into on her way out.

"Ezra Clybourn. Are you going to explain to me exactly what that phone call was about yesterday?"

He sat on the four wheeler for a moment, his thumb mindlessly flipping the gas lever, while his brain, maybe in fight or flight mode, encouraged him to turn tail and get out of there. It wasn't too late.

But, he stood, flinging one leg over the seat, and landing on the ground and striding around the car where he stood at the front of the two vehicles parked in front of the house. Alaska had gotten out of one, and she had a shy smile on her face, like she was expecting her husband-to-be, to look happy to see her, and to greet her, since he hadn't seen her all day, and it was their wedding day.

"Sondra. I can't believe you drove eight hours to get here."

"After that phone call, I'd be a fool not to. What were you thinking?" She looked around, her eyes skimming over Alaska, dismissing her as unimportant, and instead she seemed thoughtful about the ranch, the buildings, and the work that was going on. "Did you think that this was going to be too hard for me? Do you think I'm not ranchers wife material?"

At that, Alaska's eyes went from him to Sondra, and they widened. It was like she was figuring out that Sondra was not just another visitor to the ranch, but had a personal connection to Ezra.

"Alaska, this is Sondra. She is...my ex-fiancé." He hated to introduce her like that, because it made it sound like he had asked her to marry him, when he hadn't.

Before he could introduce Alaska, Sondra spoke. "Ezra. You and I need to talk. You can't keep putting me off. And you're going to have to open your mouth and speak actual words. You can't just... Ignore me."

"Alaska and I are getting married today."

That probably wasn't the best way to say it, but he knew he wasn't going to be any good at it.

Lord? Maybe I should just give up trying to have anything to do with women.

He'd already tried that. And then somehow Sondra had gotten entangled with him, and they'd ended up engaged.

"What?" Sondra said, sounding shocked and angry and like she wanted to grab a hold of someone and... He wasn't sure, but he took a step closer, feeling like he needed to protect Alaska. Which was hilarious, considering that Alaska was tiny, but scrappy, and could probably take him down if she wanted to. She ran with those kinds of people. Where Sondra was soft and probably had never balled her hand up into a fist in her life before, let alone thought about getting into some kind of physical fight.

He didn't answer her, but just stood there. Honestly, he had no idea what to say.

"Maybe you two need some time alone," Alaska said, and she sounded sad. Humble.

"You and I are leaving. We're going to the courthouse. We have an appointment at two o'clock."

"It sounds to me like you and Sondra have some things to talk about first." Alaska's eyes met his, and then she lowered them before she closed her door, and Ezra held his breath while she walked past Sondra to the front of the car.

Bernadine had not gotten out of her car, and Alaska walked around to where she had rolled her window down.

"Thank you. If you ever do that again, I'd love to help."

"I'll be in touch. It sounds to me like you have your hands full for now. Call me later."

At that, a small smile curled up Alaska's lips before she nodded.

"I will. Maybe not today. It looks like it's going to be... Complicated."

"Don't be afraid to allow Nelda to keep your kids. She loves them, and she'll be good with them."

Alaska nodded, and Bernadine put the car in reverse and started to back away.

"I'm going to go see where Nelda is." Alaska tossed that out as she walked by him, not stopping.

"Alaska." He didn't mean to have her name come out the way it did. He kind of barked it, like he was giving an order, like he wanted her to stop. But he did, and it worked, because she stopped mid stride, and turned to look at him.

The look on her face was part hurt, part inquiry, and part stubborn defiance. Like she wasn't going to allow someone like him to hurt her. But he had, he knew.

He should have told her about Sondra, should have told her that he was engaged, or at least she thought he was engaged, and explained everything. Explained it so that she understood.

He swallowed. He hated it when he did stupid stuff like this and wished he was back out, chasing cows or fixing fence or standing in a thunderstorm digging a ditch. Any of that would be better than what he was doing right now.

"Talk to Sondra first. Then you and I will figure things out." She didn't wait for him to give any more orders, and maybe she knew nothing would be forthcoming since his mouth now seemed to be opening and closing like he couldn't figure out what to say, which was exactly right.

"Don't leave." For some reason, it scared him to think that she might get someone to take her away from there. He didn't just want to help her, although he would have said that was the dominant motivation behind everything he was doing. But there was something about her, something that he didn't want to lose.

"I won't. Not until I talk to you." She sounded reluctant to say that, but he was pretty sure that once she said the words, she wouldn't go back on her word. He wasn't sure why he thought she would keep it, since he didn't know her that well, but... Maybe it was the responsible way that she had put together Ellen and Travis's wedding, the way she had done everything that needed to be done, and the few things that went wrong, she stepped up and took responsibility for.

Someone who could take responsibility for things when they didn't go right was a person of character in his book.

It was funny, because he never really thought about that before.

He watched as she started walking and went up the steps and disappeared into the farmhouse.

She hadn't even been there a week, and it already seemed like she belonged there, like it was home. Even though their home was going to be the smaller house behind it.

She just belonged at Sweet View Ranch, or maybe more accurately, she belonged with him.

He shoved a hand in his pocket, as the door closed behind her and she disappeared from sight. He turned to Sondra.

"Ezra. You're not actually marrying that...druggie, are you?"

He snorted. Why would she have called Alaska a druggie? She had no clue about Alaska's past. Was it the tattoos? The piercings? The thin frame?

It couldn't be anything else. To him, when he looked at Alaska, he saw a glow about her, something that told him that she had met Jesus, and she was walking with Him.

It might be a new relationship, and she might not be perfect, but he could see the effort.

He was pretty sure Sondra was a Christian too. She claimed to be, but right now he wasn't feeling it. Not that he relied on his feelings for much of anything.

"Yeah. I'm maybe a little crazy to say so, but I'm looking forward to it."

That probably wasn't the confession that he should have made to Sondra. Her brows drew down, and anger entered her eyes as they narrowed, and she put both hands on her hips.

"Do you think you could have said something to me? How long were you going to string me along?"

"I told you as soon as I knew. Things have gone...quickly."

"Do you have some kind of drug lord threatening you somehow? Because honest-to-goodness, Ezra, that is the only way I can figure out why someone like you would marry someone like her."

"Yeah, I guess I am kind of blessed that she agreed to marry me. I don't deserve her." He found that those words were true. Look at him now, bumbling everything, and not treating Alaska nearly the way she deserved to be treated, and yet... She hadn't told him that she was breaking up with him. At least not yet. Not that they were even together. They just decided to get married.

"Ezra. Are you going to throw away everything that we have? Everything that we worked for? All the plans and dreams that you and I have built, just to marry...that?"

"I'm sorry. I should have... Spoken up sooner. You're right." He spoke that last quickly as she opened her mouth, likely to tell him that was exactly what she was saying.

"I would say that you should have. How long were you going to drag me along?"

"I told you. As soon as I knew, I told you."

"You mean to tell me that you just decided yesterday to marry her and you were going to do it today?" She rolled her eyes. "Ezra. You forget that I've known you forever. You're not a spur of the moment person. You and I have been engaged for... Three years? Something like that." She waved her hand dismissively, but he wasn't fooled. Sondra kept track of dates. She knew exactly, down to the day, and possibly the hour and minute, how long they'd been engaged.

"You're just going to let all that go for someone that you... I assume just met?" She narrowed her eyes. "How long have you known her?"

"Less than a week." He almost closed his eyes against the onslaught he knew was coming. It felt like he was being buffered in a storm. He would rather be naked and lost in a North Dakota snowstorm, then be facing Sondra right now.

"Less than a week?" she shrieked, her voice shrill. "Ezra Clybourn, if your parents were alive they would die."

She didn't seem to see the irony in that statement, and the mention of his parents sent a small pain through his chest. He wished they were alive. His mom would love Alaska. His dad would encourage him to do the right thing, to do what he thought God wanted him to do, and Ezra was sure that marrying Alaska, as crazy as it was, was the exact right thing.

"I think they would like her. The same way they liked you."

That shut her up. Her mouth, which had been open, probably to give him another piece of her mind, snapped shut.

"I loved your parents so much." Her voice wobbled a bit, and he set up a new prayer. *Lord, please don't let her cry.*

"I think everybody who knew them loved them." He took a breath. "Sorry. You're right. I shouldn't have allowed this to go on as long as it did. I just... I guess I was lazy. I knew it was going to involve confrontation, and I didn't want that to happen. So I just let it go. You know as well as I do that you and I aren't compatible at all. The things you love, aren't things I care for. Not even a little bit." And that was a major understatement. He didn't even own a TV, and that seemed to be what her life revolved around. Whatever came off the screen, defined her. "And you have a whole world that I'm not in. You deserve someone who wants to be with you, and wants to be in that world, wants to share those things with you."

"I want it to be you!" she said, and her lip trembled. "I wanted all that to be you. Why can't you do that? You know it! You know what's right. You know you're supposed to be interested in the things I'm interested in, and you know that I've tried hard to learn to be a ranch girl. I watched seven different shows about people who live on ranches, and I know everything there is to know about it. I just need to put it into practice, but you would never take the time to show me."

He shoved his other hand in his pocket and looked away. She was right. She had wanted to be a part of the farm. Part of the ranch in Wyoming. And he hadn't wanted to spend the time with her. He'd always come up with some excuse, or just hadn't told her what he was doing. Or pawned her off on one of his sisters. Being with Sondra wasn't like being with Alaska. He wanted to be with Alaska. Even now, she'd disappeared inside the house, and he wanted to go to her, touch her, make sure everything was okay between them.

With Sondra, he was just putting in time until she dismissed him, and he didn't have to talk to her anymore.

"I'm sorry. You're right. We didn't work out, and it was all my fault. All me."

"We can fix it. We can make this work. We could have something really good together. Just like any famous movie star romance." She named a couple of names, they meant nothing to him, but he assumed that they were from the movies, or TV or something, people who had gotten together and famously. Whether in real life, or whether make-believe, he wasn't sure.

"Sondra. No. You... Are welcome to be a part of our family if that's what you want." With insight that he didn't typically possess, he suddenly realized that was probably what she wanted more than anything. She didn't have a big family, and she had always loved his. It wasn't him that she wanted as much as she wanted to be a part of his family. "There's a place for you here if you want." He shut his mouth. Maybe he shouldn't have said that. It might make Alaska uncomfortable to have Sondra around.

But why would it? Alaska had nothing to fear from her. He was telling Sondra now that he couldn't be with her because he wanted to be with Alaska. There shouldn't be any trouble at all. No. Alaska would totally understand.

"You don't mean that. You don't want me here." A tear rolled down Sondra's cheek, one single tear, almost as though she had orchestrated it. Maybe she had. He would have no idea how to tell, or what to do even if it was fake, or if it was real.

He didn't know what to say. He didn't know how to comfort her, didn't know how to get away from her, didn't know how to un-entangle himself from this. He'd apologized, told her it was all his fault, and...it hadn't seemed to make a difference.

"Sondra, I think you'd better come with me." Asher spoke from behind Ezra.

Ezra turned. He hadn't realized Asher had come up to him.

"Why? I don't want to go with you. I want you to talk sense into Ezra. Did you see the thing that he says he's going to marry?"

"Alaska has been a nice lady. I think we ought to be respectful to her, especially since my brother is most likely going to be married to her by the end of the day." Asher's tone didn't hold any emotion at all. It sounded completely flat.

But Ezra felt something, some kind of emotion rolling off him.

Could Asher have a crush on Sondra? Could he have stood back because he thought that Ezra and Sondra were meant to be together?

That seemed like a leap of logic, and Ezra dismissed it immediately.

"They're not going to be if I have any say in it. Ezra owes me a lot more than a breakup over the phone and just walking away without trying to repair anything in our relationship."

"You and Ezra don't really have a relationship. And if you think that's a relationship, that's a problem on your part." Asher didn't pull any punches, and Ezra thought that Sondra would probably burst into tears. So he was shocked whenever she took three steps toward Asher, with her arms crossed over her chest, and she practically drilled him with her eyes.

"How dare you lecture me on what a relationship is. You have nothing. You've never even been out with the girl. You have no idea of how to handle women, or how to have a relationship. You, Asher Clybourn, have a lot to learn."

"I suppose you're right." Asher pressed his lips together, then he looked back up at Sondra. "Maybe you could teach me a thing or two."

"As soon as I give your brother a piece of my mind, I'll take you off by your ear, and give you about fifteen things you can work on immediately to make you a better person."

"Come on. We'll leave Ezra here. He's got some things he needs to do, and it sounds to me like you and I have some work we need to do."

Sondra's mouth opened and closed, and Ezra hid a smile. It was kind of nice to see her at a loss for words for once. Typically it was him that was ended up scrounging around trying to figure out what he could say when he was around Sondra. But Asher had rendered her speechless. It was an interesting sight.

Finally, she turned to him, lifted her brows and said, "You just go ahead on the path you're on. You're going to regret it, mark my words. And then, when you come crawling back to me, I will remind you of this very conversation, and how I tried to talk you out of it, and how you refused to listen."

"All right. I suppose, if I ever come crawling back to you, you owe me that. And I'll listen to you."

She harrumphed, like his humble attitude wasn't doing anything for her, and then she grabbed a hold of Asher's arm.

"Let's go."

Ezra's brows went up. Even though Asher had offered, and Sondra had said that she was going to go, he couldn't believe that it was that easy. That Asher just told her, and she grabbed his arm and wanted to start walking.

Ezra tried to figure out what in the world Asher had done that he hadn't, but like most things with women, he really had no clue.

He wanted to say, "thanks bro," but he didn't. He didn't want to do anything that might make Sondra turn around and spew more of her wrath on him.

Sondra took two steps, and Asher walked beside her, then his head turned, and he met Ezra's eyes.

Ezra mouthed, "thank you" but he didn't smile. And neither did Asher.

He wasn't sure what he read on Asher's face, but he thought that maybe his first instinct, the one that said that Asher had a crush on Sondra he'd been hiding, seemed even more probable.

"We'll be at my cabin in Montana," Asher said, and to Ezra's surprise that made Sondra stop.

Ezra glanced at Sondra, and then back at his brother. "How long?"

"I guess as long as it takes for her to teach me what I need to know," he said, one side of his mouth going up.

He supposed Asher just wanted him to know that Sondra would be out of the picture. Even though they needed Asher's help on the farm, Ezra understood that Asher was trying to help.

"You have a cabin in Montana?" Sondra asked, her eyes going wide. "Why that's just like the TV show, Cabin in the Mountain. Have you seen it?"

Asher huffed out a laugh, and shook his head no, his eyes on Sondra. And there was something in them, something... Something Ezra knew had never been in *his* eyes when he looked at Sondra. Admiration.

He wasn't sure what Asher found to admire, but the idea that he did, that Sondra would be okay, made the tight knot that had been in his chest since he'd seen her car pulling in the driveway loosen

He made a mess of everything. He always seemed to do that, but it looked like maybe the Lord was working things out.

Now, all he had to do was go and let Alaska know that it was time for them to get married. With Sondra out of the picture, Alaska would be fine, and everything would be just the way it was.

Chapter Fourteen

Ezra stepped in the house, not feeling very good about himself. Anyone who looked at him, would think that he had his life together. He knew he gave that impression, but he felt like he'd really messed things up. At least personally. Sure, the ranch was struggling, but that was life. A person didn't expect to step into adulthood and become a success the first time they did something. They expected to work and strive and see success and failure throughout their lifetime.

But personally... He was almost forty. He should have something together by now, but he didn't. It didn't feel like he was even close to having things figured out, even though he was supposed to get married today.

"Alaska?" he called, when he didn't see her in the living room, nor the study. He thought about going upstairs, but figured that she probably wouldn't be there. She'd been up to get his things out of his room the day before, but there was nothing for her up there.

He tried to think of where she would be, and the little house next door was the only place he could come up with. There really wasn't any place for her anywhere. She hadn't been on the ranch long enough to have a place of her own. A place where she loved, one that she sought out in her private moments.

For him, there was a little grove of cottonwood trees about a mile from the barn. It was right beside the creek, and while the creek was quiet and kind of meandering and slow, it still gave him a sense of peace to see it flow and just feel the breeze, watch the leaves rustle along with the grass, and sit by the water.

Suddenly, he wanted to take Alaska to his spot. To show it to her.

That was really getting the cart ahead of the horse. He needed to figure out how to develop a relationship with her, and...that was going to take time. He was going to have to make time, along with all the other things that he needed to do.

He didn't know how.

He walked through the back door, and to his surprise, Alaska sat on the steps, her feet pulled up tight against her chest, and her arms wrapped around them.

Lord, please don't let her be crying.

He didn't know what he was going to do if she was. He was so far out of his league with all of this, he wished he'd just kept his mouth shut, and tried to figure out another way to protect her.

It wasn't too late. They could decide not to get married. But there was a part of him that rebelled against that.

"Alaska?" He spoke softly, not wanting to startle her, but she must have figured out it was him when she heard the door opening, because she didn't startle, or even turn around.

"Are you not talking to me?" he asked, unsure.

"Should I be?" she asked, and her voice sounded fatalistic.

"I'd like it if you were. We can't really work anything out if one of us isn't speaking to the other."

"Well, considering that we had all of one conversation in our entire relationship, I suppose talking might be a good start." She took a breath. He could see her back rise, and then fall as she blew it out. "Maybe we shouldn't get married."

It sounded like she didn't want to say it, or maybe that was just him hoping.

"Can I sit down?"

She looked beside her, as though judging whether or not there was enough space on the step for him.

Her hands released her legs, and she scooted over to allow room for him.

"Thanks," he said, sitting down beside her.

Lord, I'm terrible at this. But every time I think about marrying Alaska, I feel like it's the right thing to do. If it is, I know you're going to work this out. I'll do my best, but you and I both know this is not something I'm good at. I suppose, since you're putting this in my lap, it's something you want me to get better at. But I don't know how.

And, as he was praying, a thought came to him.

Be honest.

What a novel idea.

He sighed. "I'm not very good at this."

"Good at what?" she asked, and he was grateful that she was at least talking to him. Some of his sisters could go days, weeks, giving him the silent treatment when they were younger. His parents never allowed it, but sometimes they could get away with doing it to him if his parents didn't figure out what they were doing. His mom and dad had been big believers in discussing things, and not pretending that nothing was wrong. He, on the other hand, would much rather pretend that nothing was wrong, and just muddle through.

"Talking to women."

"I suppose that is pretty obvious, considering that you had a fiancé you didn't tell me about, even though you and I were supposed to get married."

"See? I told you I wasn't any good."

She laughed a little. And he felt like maybe that was the first hurdle. That she wasn't completely cold to him. He could make her laugh a little. He wasn't exactly known as someone who was jovial and funny, but it made him happy to hear Alaska laugh. She had a slightly husky laugh, one that moved over him smooth, like warm honey.

"I like to hear you laugh."

"I didn't know we knew each other well enough to know what we liked about each other."

"That bothers you?"

"It didn't. But maybe it should. I didn't like the surprise of finding out that you had a fiancé. And I really didn't like the surprise of seeing her today, and seeing that she thought she still had a claim on you. Considering that we're supposed to be in Rockerton at the courthouse, it just feels...not right."

Probably because it wasn't right. "Again, that's my fault."

He didn't ask her where her children were, although it occurred to him just then to wonder. Probably Nelda had expected them to be gone all day, and she had either taken them to her house, or gone somewhere with them.

"Does that happen often?" Alaska asked. Then, she wrapped her arms around her legs again, and leaned forward just a bit, as though protecting herself. "I know I really don't have the right to ask. I —"

"You do."

"No. You're marrying me because of pity. To protect me. To protect my children and give them a life. I should be grateful, not demanding fidelity."

"You have to demand fidelity. That's a given in marriage. It's definitely something I owe you, if I'm going to make you my wife."

"Like you owed Sondra?"

"I told you, that's different."

"What if I start going around saying something, and start believing that it's true, are you going to correct me?"

"I guess I should. I shouldn't just let things go. I... I'm bad at that, because I know this kind of thing...what you and I were talking about... It's stuff that isn't concrete. It makes me feel squirmy inside." Squirmy wasn't exactly a manly word, but he didn't have another word to use. He couldn't think of anything else that was applicable.

"I guess I can understand that. The idea of this ranch, of me being on it, I feel like I don't know anything. I mean, I wanted to storm away somewhere, but I didn't even know where I could go. You know?"

"That's funny. I was thinking as I was walking in the house that there's a spot that I wanted to show you. It's my favorite spot on the farm."

"I'd like to see it." Her eyes dropped down. "You know, you're not the only one who's not any good at this kind of thing."

"Are you trying to tell me that you're not either?" He found that hard to believe. Weren't women naturals at relationships? And the whole controversy between men and women was because women were good at it and men weren't, right?

"Yeah. That's exactly what I'm saying. I don't typically have good relationships. I guess I have a tendency to fall for men who are unavailable."

"What do you mean?"

"I mean the father of my two children was married."

"I'm not sure I knew that."

"Yeah. That says a whole lot about me, doesn't it?"

"I don't think you're that person anymore." He spoke slowly. Hoping that was true. He didn't want to get married to someone who didn't think that marriage vows were sacred.

"No. That was before Jesus. I hope I'm not that person anymore, but once you've done something, sometimes you're just afraid that you're going to continue to do that same thing, even though you don't want to. Maybe you don't have that problem."

"No. I do. I want to be the kind of person who is able to talk to people, but every time I try, I seem to say something stupid. It doesn't matter how many times I think to myself I don't want to open my mouth unless I know what's coming out is going to be beneficial, I just...this is not the only time where I had that problem."

"Yeah. You don't seem like you talk a lot."

"I don't really need to."

"I think sometimes your wife wants you to talk to her."

"Oh does she?" He smiled a little. She wasn't even his wife yet.

"I think she will."

Just talking about it made him eager to get in the truck and head to Rockerton. He wanted her to be his wife. He couldn't even explain exactly why. He thought about the danger, and looked both ways, not that he would have any idea of how to spot danger, unless he saw someone coming toward him in a threatening way.

"You know, maybe I'm out of my league with the idea that I can protect you. I'm a rancher. I fix stuff, grow things, work cattle. I don't have any detective skills or great protective skills. I just... I just hope to keep an eye on things. I guess."

"Like watching a cow that's getting ready to have a baby?"

He laughed. "I guess. I do that. Although our cows are bred to be able to calve on their own and don't usually need human help.

"I have no idea."

"Hey. You'll learn." He put a hand on her arm, reaching out because she sounded so despondent. He could understand the feeling. It occurred to him to try to reach her that way. Through their weaknesses. "You don't know anything about ranching. I don't know anything about relationships. I don't know anything about being a husband. I don't know anything about...talking. Not when we're talking about relationships." He huffed out a laugh. "I don't even know how to tell you what I don't know how to do."

She laughed along with him. "You're doing a good job. You know, even more important than doing it right, is just showing that you care and when you try, it shows. And I suppose I would rather see that than having you know how to do everything exactly right, but feel like there's no heart behind it. Does that make sense?"

"Yeah. I think that's the easy way out. You want to just put in the time, get it done, so you don't have to worry about it, and can cross it off your list. But a relationship really isn't like that. It's not something you can cross off. At least, I guess I'm figuring that out. But, I always did try to have a good relationship with my siblings, and my parents modeled that. I... Didn't care about having a good relationship with Sondra. So, maybe that allowed me to get into some bad habits."

"Maybe," she said, and it sounded noncommittal.

"What's the matter? Why did you sound so much different when I talked about Sondra?"

At first he didn't think she was going to answer him. Then he thought maybe he was being dense. Maybe she thought he knew the answer and was just asking to be smart.

"Like you don't know."

"I really don't. I know that I should know more than what I do, but this is not the kind of thing that I focused on. Will you help me?"

"I'm sorry. It just seems like it would be common sense, but then I suppose there's going to be a lot of things on the ranch that to you are common sense, and to me are new and don't make any sense at all."

"That's fair." He figured she was probably right.

"So, I don't really like hearing about Sondra. You were engaged for goodness sake. And you're supposed to marry me. And you didn't break up with her until yesterday. It kind of makes me feel like you want to hang on, and when you bring her up, it makes me feel like you're thinking about her. If you're talking about her, and holding onto her, then I think that maybe you and I shouldn't get married because you still have a thing for Sondra."

"Trust me. I do not have a thing for Sondra. I never really did. I just..." He paused. He wanted to say that he just didn't really care who he married. He wanted to get married. He wanted to start a family. He wanted to be like his parents, but pretty much any woman would do, except he could never really be happy spending time with Sondra.

Something told him that wouldn't sound good to Alaska, and he was finding that it wasn't completely true anymore. He wanted to spend time with Alaska, wanted to be around her. Wanted to talk to her. And that was a first.

"I know this is crazy, because we don't know each other very well, but until I met you, I didn't really care which woman I was with. They all seemed pretty much the same." There. Maybe he shouldn't have said that, but maybe it would help too. Because, there was a difference with her.

"Until me? Are you just saying that?"

"I think if there's one thing you can say about me, it's that I don't just say things. I try really hard to mean what I say, and maybe that's part of the reason why talking about relationships is so hard for me. I can't just spout off pretty words that don't mean anything. If there's no meaning behind them, if I don't mean it, then it's hard for me to say." He realized his hand was still on her arm, and he wanted to move it up and down, lightly touching her skin, maybe a little soothing, but he made himself be still.

"I always think of my brother, Caleb, as being charming. But I know that sometimes he says things that he doesn't really mean just to make someone else feel good. To me that's charming, but it's not really right. Part of me rebels at the idea that you say things to someone just to make them smile. Not because you mean it. Does that make sense?"

"Yeah. I suppose it does. I guess I've been around people most of my life who say a lot of things that they don't mean. Will say anything to get what they want, whether it's true or not."

"That's definitely not me."

"I appreciate that," she said, lifting her brows and looking at him with sincerity in her gaze. "But I'm not used to it."

"So maybe you're not going to hear words that you expect to hear?"

"Yeah. Maybe I just need to get used to the fact that you're not always going to say what I think you should be saying. And that's a good thing."

"That sounds like a deal to me. Maybe you can... Let me know if there's something that I should be saying that I'm not?"

"That's a little awkward. And mostly because if someone doesn't say something, you don't want to have to tell them to. For example, I feel like you should care about me, and ask me how I am, without me having to tell you that you're supposed to ask me how I am. Otherwise, if I have to prompt you, it makes it seem like you're doing it because you have to, rather than because you want to. Which still means that you don't care, even though you asked. Does that make sense?"

"Or maybe you're just reminding me, because as you said that, it made me realize that I didn't really ask you how you were. And I do care. I want to know. How are you?"

She smiled, and he hadn't really meant for it to be funny. It was true. He hadn't really thought about how she was. Other than making sure that she was safe. But, for some reason, he wanted to know everything about her. The more time he spent with her, the more interesting she seemed to him.

"I'm fine."

"I have enough sisters to know that fine means the opposite in that context."

She laughed, as he had intended. It was just coincidence that not very long ago that his sisters were having a discussion about how people said they were fine when they really weren't, and it was usually women.

"I can't argue with that. That's true. I'm fine is the standard answer, and if that's all a person can think of to say, then they're probably not fine."

"Women. I think men probably are fine."

She huffed out another laugh, and he moved his hand, running it up her arm to her shoulder, and then saying, "Is it okay touching you? I... I just want to."

Chapter Fifteen

"That's... Weird. But nice."

"Weird?" Ezra asked. "I don't think that's a good thing?"

"Yeah. I think that's a good thing. I... Because it's not the kind of thing a man usually talks to me about. Usually he just touches me, and I don't really get any say in it." Alaska shivered.

"You should. You should have all the say."

"All of it?" Her brows furrowed. "Shouldn't it be the two of us deciding together?"

"If that's your way of asking me if I want you to touch me, the answer is yes."

She laughed. "That wasn't exactly what I was asking, but...that's good to know."

They sat there for a moment, his hand on her shoulder, and he felt a little awkward.

"I can't help but notice that you didn't move to touch me. That... raises questions for me."

"It does?"

"Sure." He wasn't sure how to explain what he wanted to know. Or... How that made him feel. He definitely wasn't used to talking about his feelings.

"What questions exactly does it raise?" she asked.

"You gave me permission to touch you, and I want to. I gave you the same permission, and you didn't move. Why?"

He felt really uncomfortable asking that. Vulnerable. Vulnerability wasn't something he was used to showing. But, he had a feeling that it was something that he was going to need to get more comfortable with in order for him to establish a bond of trust between him and his wife.

"Maybe because I didn't believe you."

"Didn't believe me?"

"That you really want me to. Or, maybe I wasn't sure how." She drew her brows down, like she wasn't sure how to explain that.

"Are you able to tell me what you mean?"

"I don't know. Maybe that you were just saying it felt good? And then, where should I touch you? On your arm? Your leg? I don't know. That isn't the kind of touching that I'm used to. It's..."

He thought he understood. That she didn't typically just touch a man for the sake of touching him. He looked away. Not moving his hand, but moving his attention for a moment, because he needed to think. Maybe he was reading it all wrong, but it seemed like to her, touching meant sex. To him...maybe, but it was more than that.

"I don't talk too much about my parents. They died in a car accident, it was more than ten years ago now. But, even then I got to spend about three decades with them. They," he grunted a little. "My sister said I look back through rose colored glasses because in my mind, my parents were perfect. I know they weren't."

"I'm never going to be perfect," she said, and she sounded defensive. That wasn't where he was going at all.

"I know. I was just... Trying to explain."

"Okay?" she said.

Where to start? He wanted her to understand where he was going with the whole touching thing.

"I loved watching my parents. I mean, when I was a teenager, especially early teens like thirteen through fifteen, it was kind of gross. But as I got older, I loved seeing how they couldn't pass each other without touching. Dad would stroke mom's hair, or tuck it back behind her ear, or rub his finger down under her hairline around her neck. That always made her shiver, and I know that's kind of a weird thing to notice about your mom, but she seemed to really like it. And he did it often. Not at night before they went to bed. It wasn't about... sex. It was like if they were beside each other, he wanted to reach out and see that she was there, he just needed to touch her. Maybe it's a little bit the way it is when you stroke your dog's head. You know? Not that I'm comparing a husband and wife to animals. But, you know your dog really enjoys your touch. And when I looked at my parents, I knew they enjoyed each other's touch. I'm sure in a sexual way, but it's a little bit weird to think of my parents in that way. Just, they always held hands. Even after twelve children, my dad would kiss the top of my mom's head, or hug her and thank her for a meal, just... Always touching."

"Those must be really nice memories. My parents were always yelling at each other. Actually, my mom was always yelling at whatever man was living with her."

"That's sad. I don't recall my parents ever fighting."

"That's impossible."

"No. I'm serious. I can't say they didn't have disagreements. They argued about the heat. Mom liked it cold in the summer, and hot in the winter. My dad was the opposite. He thought people should be acclimated to the weather, and if it was hot outside, it shouldn't be super cold in the house. Anyway, that is something they argued about. Mom would turn the heat up or down, and dad would do the opposite. They'd have big, long discussions using logical arguments as to why they were right. It was kind of funny to listen to them." He remembered that while they discussed it, they were never mad at each other. They might have been very vocal in their opinions, but they had figured out how to disagree with each other without disliking each other.

"That almost seems like a daydream. A fairytale. I can't imagine a marriage like that."

"That's how I want my marriage to be. I... I want to be able to talk to my wife, which I suppose is why I'm putting such an effort into it."

"I appreciate it."

"But I want us to be able to disagree without hating each other. Or... I guess my parents just always thought best about each other."

"That's a talent. I don't know if I think the best of anyone all the time. Everyone has a bad side."

"I know I do. I suppose you do too, but maybe... Maybe I'll just try to put blinders on so I don't see that side."

"Isn't that a little bit like sticking your head in the sand and not facing reality?"

"Or maybe it's deciding what you're going to focus on."

"Oh."

"I suppose it's a little bit of positive thinking, but if you're married to someone, shouldn't you look for the best?"

"I guess I never really thought about it. I wasn't raised the way you were."

"What kind of relationship do you want?"

"I guess I just want a relationship where my husband takes care of me, takes care of my children, and while I expected to hold down a job, I just wanted him to pull his weight too, you know? Like the man is supposed to be the provider or whatever, and the woman takes care of the kids, although it would be nice to have help with that."

"I think that's biblical. The Bible does command the man to be the protector, and it actually says that the man who won't provide for his own house is worse than an infidel."

"Does it really?" she asked, and then she said, "What's an infidel?"

He laughed. "An unbeliever, I guess."

"All right."

"And it does say that the women are supposed to be the keepers at home. That she is supposed to care for the children. But, I do think that it takes both the husband and wife, a mom and dad, not just to keep the house, but raise the children. It's just...working together, figuring out what works for both of you. And not being so rigid and expecting everything that you think is the only right way, and that anything anyone else thinks is absolutely wrong."

"I suppose that's bad for anything."

"Yeah."

"Do you think we could ever have a relationship like your parents?" she asked, and her fingers moved a little, twitching, like maybe she was thinking about moving them to touch him, but she just couldn't quite get there.

"I hope. I guess that's my ideal. Not that I'm holding you to a high standard, because I really think that their relationship was because of my dad. I mean, my mom was an awesome woman, and I loved her. But, my dad was the one who made sure that they got along. He was the first to apologize. He was the leader. There was never any question about whether or not he was the head of our home. But he didn't lead with such an iron fist that my mom was browbeaten into submission."

"Submission. That's a disgusting word."

"Is it?"

"Yeah. It's like slaves or something. Like, back in the olden days when the woman was a slave to the man."

He didn't say anything about that. Submission was biblical. Both man submitting to God, and a wife submitting to her husband. It was the Bible way. But he didn't want to argue about it now. Although, he supposed now was the best time. If his wife wasn't going to be submissive... Did he want to get married?

He probably shouldn't.

"I guess the most important thing to me is to have a marriage based on biblical principles."

"You mean, using the Bible to make decisions?"

"Sure. If God lays out the way He wants a marriage to be in the Bible, shouldn't we follow that?"

"Isn't that old-fashioned?"

"Do you think God is with the program? Don't you think His principles are timeless?"

"That's a good point." She seemed to be considering that, and he didn't say anything else. Maybe he shouldn't consider marriage to someone who didn't believe everything he did, but if they could agree on that one thing, that the Bible was the authority between them, then everything else would fall into place, if they were both striving to live toward that. He felt like that was the most important thing to establish. Whether or not a person was submissive, or anything else, all fell under the umbrella of believing the Bible was the inspired Word of God.

"I guess I haven't been a Christian long enough to know everything the Bible says, but I do want to follow it. If God took the time to write down everything He thought we should do, I suppose it would be foolish of me to say that I was Christian, that I believed God, but I don't do everything He tells me to because... I just don't want to, I guess."

"That's all you needed to say to convince me."

She laughed a little. "Really?"

"Yeah. As long as we believe the Bible is the final authority, I don't think we'll have any trouble."

"You mean, the Bible will let us know what temperature we should set our thermostat?"

He laughed. And she smiled, like she liked the sound of his laughter. Maybe the way he liked the sound of hers.

"Actually, if you want to get technical about it, it does."

"Really?"

"Sure. The Bible says the man is the head of the house, so I get to decide what temperature the thermostat is set."

"That doesn't really sound fair."

"Don't ever say that God's way is fair. Not in our eyes anyway, but there is one caveat."

"Caveat?"

"The Bible says that the man is the head, the authority over the woman, but the man has a command."

"Okay."

"The command is to love the woman as he loves himself. Now, I have a dilemma. Do I put the thermostat where I want it, because I am the leader of the home? Or do I put the thermostat where you want it, because I love you as I love myself?"

"Well. That's tough." She grinned. Smiling at the silliness of the example, but he figured she probably understood what he was saying.

"So, if you're truly going to be a man of God, you have to balance the fact that you are the authority with the fact that you are commanded to love me."

"Yeah. Not just that, but I'm also commanded to give you honor, as the weaker vessel. Those are the Bible's words, not mine."

"So maybe that just means I'm physically not as strong as you are?"

"I don't know. Adam wasn't deceived by the serpent, Eve was. I'm not sure exactly what that means, but possibly it means that women are more easily led astray than men are. We have a tendency to be more analytical about things, while women seem to be led by their feelings."

"And sometimes our feelings are right."

"And sometimes they're not. But the data doesn't lie."

She didn't say anything, and he wondered if maybe he pushed her a little bit too far. He and his sisters had had more than one discussion about exactly that. And, while his sisters had lots of things to say, they couldn't argue with the fact that Adam, the man, hadn't been the one that had been deceived.

"You know, I don't know if we solved anything just now, but just the fact that you took the time to come out here and sit down with me and talk to me, about things that don't even really matter maybe, but you just... Instead of working, instead of pushing to go make our appointment, you gave me the time I need. That... Means a lot. Thank you for your attention, and your time."

He nodded. "I guess what we were talking about, the man being the provider, I feel that pretty heavy, like I need to provide for you for our children. For my family and my siblings. That's not going to go away once we get married."

"I don't expect it to."

"So I want to work hard. If I spend a lot of time on the ranch and ranch making it successful, part of it is for me. My reputation, because people have loaned me money, and I need to make sure that I prove myself worthy of the trust they gave me, but a lot of it is because I'm driven to take care of the people who depend on me. That's my siblings, and I assume that would be my wife and our children." He made sure to say *our* children, not her. Because he didn't want there to be a "her children" and "his children" or "their children", and there to be some kind of difference. If they were married, any children between them would be theirs.

In his eyes anyway.

"Where are the kids?" He felt a little bit odd asking, since they hadn't discussed it. Maybe they should.

"Nelda has them. She took them to the playground in Sweet Water this morning, and they're sleeping right now."

"Here?" he said, indicating the small house that was just a few steps away from the larger one.

"She took them to her house. I... I don't really know where that is."

"I'm going to have to give you a tour of the farm. But, are we still getting married?" He held his breath, hoping that her answer was still yes. He didn't know why. He probably should have cold feet and want her to as well.

But he didn't. Now more than anything, he wanted her to continue on. He felt like they made some major strides, knowing that they agreed on some things, and while he didn't expect things to go perfectly, he had to admit he was excited about moving forward.

"Yeah. Unless you changed your mind?" she said, and insecurity laced her words.

"No. Absolutely not. I said I would, and I meant it, and...even more than that," he hurried to add, when she opened her mouth. He thought she was going to say that him doing something out of duty wasn't the same as him doing something because he wanted to. He understood the distinction between those two things. After all, he didn't want her to do anything for him out of duty. He wanted her to do it out of... Love.

He tucked that thought away to think about later, or never. Because he hadn't really thought that he was susceptible to the idea of love, but he found himself wanting something more than just duty from Alaska.

"Even more than that, I want to. Now that we've talked, I want it more than I did before we did. I'm glad you made me."

"I didn't make you. You came out here and sat down."

"All right. I'm glad we did too. I feel a lot better."

"Had you been scared?" He kinda thought that maybe that would be a natural feeling, although it wasn't one he felt.

"No. I wasn't scared. I was... Feeling like I should do the right thing and call it off, because a woman like Sondra is the kind of woman that I would expect a man like you to be with."

"I would expect that I should be with the woman God wants me to be with. I think that's you."

She closed her mouth and didn't say anything more. Maybe he'd been too strong for her. Maybe she didn't like the idea that he thought that God was putting them together. Maybe that was too woo-woo for her. He definitely had a line where things got too woo-woo for him.

"I need to change, and then I'm ready to go."

"All right. I suppose I'll go... Wash my hands. I don't have a dress."

"You don't need one. You look fine in what you're wearing. I smell like cows, and I'm dirty, too, or I'd wear this. What I put on is going to be just like this, only probably a different color." He pointed to his shirt.

She laughed. "You mean you don't have a deep wardrobe full of expensive suits that you can just yank out any time you decide to get married?"

"No. I don't."

"Good. Because you better not decide to get married again."

"I think I might have mentioned this will be the first and only time." He supposed that if, God forbid, something would happen to Alaska, he might get married again, but he doubted it. He was most definitely a one woman man kind of person. He knew a person should never say never, but for him, one woman in a lifetime was enough.

"All right, is ten minutes enough time?" he said, standing, and holding his hand out for her to help her up. She looked at it for a moment, and then put her hand in his. "Plenty of time," she said, sounding calm. Although maybe a little breathless. Whether it was from standing, or whether it was from nervousness that she was hiding, he wasn't sure. Or, maybe standing so close to him had a similar effect on her as it did on him. He... Wanted to be closer, and at the same time felt nervous and a little uncertain.

"I guess I need to ask you where my clothes are. I noticed last night that you'd taken everything except for this outfit that you left on my dresser. I assume the rest of them are over there?" he said, nodding his head at the little house.

"Yeah. You told me to move everything, so I did. But I wasn't sure where you were going to sleep last night, so I left an outfit for you just in case."

"I appreciate your thoughtfulness. I'll be in the little house tonight, although... I figured I would sleep on the couch."

"You don't have to," she said quickly.

"I guess we can talk about it."

While he felt it was important for them to get married so that she would have the protection of his family, and have the safety of the ranch, he didn't know that their relationship necessarily had to go that fast.

There would be plenty of time to talk about that both on the way to Rockerton and on the way home, so he didn't say anything more. But, he lifted his hand and held it out, and she looked at it for a moment before she slipped her hand back into his, and they held hands as they walked to the little house. It was a start. A good one.

Chapter Sixteen

Alaska sat beside Ezra in his truck, her fingers twisting in her lap. She did feel a lot better since he had taken the time to sit down with her, and just chat. In her experience, men didn't typically want to waste time chatting. They either wanted something physical, or they wanted to do something, not talk. The fact that Ezra just casually sat down, and did something that was hard for him, for her, and that was the only reason. Just because of her. It almost made her forget that he had been engaged yesterday, and that she had been confronted by his jilted fiancée that morning.

It was the kind of drama she wouldn't have expected from a man like Ezra. It had made her question everything she thought. Not that she wanted to look a gift horse in the mouth, because she knew Ezra was giving her far more than she deserved. And she wasn't quite sure why.

From talking to him, she almost felt like he wasn't sure why, either. That's what he had said before, but she kind of believed it now. He wasn't a man who was used to doing things based on what he felt, but he was a man who tried to do what God wanted. And that was the key. For some reason, he felt that God wanted him to marry her, and so he was doing it, but he hinted that he wanted to. Because she didn't want him to do something just because he felt he had to. Not for her. She wanted more. Even as she recognized that it was ridiculous. She should be grateful for what she had. Thankful that he had given her as much as what he had, and not demand more.

And for some reason, that made her remember something she needed to do. She already didn't feel worthy of Ezra, or what he had offered her, but she felt especially guilty when she thought about her past actions, and how they impacted other people's lives. Including her children's.

"Can we stop somewhere?" she blurted out, before she lost her nerve. Not only did she have to have the nerve to go do what she needed to do, but she had to ask Ezra, and remind him of how terrible her past was. It could be the thing that made him decide that he didn't want to be married to her after all.

"Uh, sure. Before or after we get married?" he asked, casually, and she didn't feel pressure, even though she knew that they were never going to make the appointment that they'd made.

"Before."

"All right. You sound like it's pretty important to you."

"It's necessary, I think. For me, but for you too. And...someone else."

"All right. I'm curious. Where do you want to go?"

"Sweet Water." She gave him the address. It wasn't a familiar one to her, although she knew it. But, it was where she needed to go today.

"I can get us to the street, then you just make sure I get to the right house."

"All right." She had driven by the house multiple times. Back when she was obsessed. To her shame.

Ezra didn't say anything more, and maybe she fell in love with him just a little bit right then, when he didn't press her, didn't demand that she explain what she wanted, but simply did what she asked, even though she hadn't told him why. For herself, she might not have been able to do what someone asked, without an explanation.

Spring in North Dakota was beautiful, with several different varieties of wild flowers blooming along the road, as they drove along, contrasting in such a pretty way with the green grass, and the blue sky, and the white puffy clouds that floated in lazy randomness. Every once in a while they passed a field where cattle grazed, and that completed the picture of the ideal country life. It was hard to believe that land had been brutally beaten by cold and snow and ice and wind all winter long. For six months at least. Now, it had emerged, breathtaking in its beauty, and seemingly carefree.

Maybe there were lessons there for her. Maybe everyone had seasons of going through trials and hardships, maybe those trials were necessary for a person to emerge, blooming more brightly than ever before.

She figured that was probably the case, and maybe this would be one of those things. This hard thing that she knew she had to do, maybe she would be better for it.

Ezra pulled down the road, she directed him to the house, an unassuming white ranch with brown shutters. There were no flowers in the yard, but there were several toys lying around, like the kids had been playing, and they'd gone straight in without putting their things away.

The way Alaska's yard often looked.

"Do you need me to come in with you?" Ezra asked as he pulled to a stop in front of the closed garage door.

"No." She drew the word out little as she thought about it. "I'd really love to have you beside me, but I do believe this is something I need to do on my own."

She didn't want to. She didn't want to do it at all, and she wanted to cling to Ezra, but, while she did believe that a spouse was someone that God gave a person so they didn't have to face life alone, so they had a companion through the hard times, she knew that having Ezra beside her would be intimidating to the person she needed to talk to.

She didn't want it to look like she was ganging up on them, and she certainly didn't want to look like she was lording it over them, or rubbing it in.

And she had to admit, part of it was she didn't want Ezra to hear what she had to say. Except, she almost asked him if he'd come. After all, maybe he *needed* to hear.

"Actually," she turned her head to look at him across the seat. "Would you mind coming, but not standing too close? I don't want to intimidate her."

He stared at her for a moment, as though rolling over in his mind what in the world she'd be talking about, but then he nodded. "If that's what you want, that's what I'll do."

She could hardly believe how easy it was. Shouldn't he argue with her? Shouldn't he give her a hard time? He definitely shouldn't just go along. She'd never been with anyone who didn't give her a hard time about pretty much everything she did. Who was willing to do things they didn't want to do without arguing or fighting. It was a good example for her, because she wondered if she was that kind of person. The kind of person who was willing to do things she didn't want to do without fussing about them.

She had to admit, she was a fusser.

It wasn't a pretty admission.

But it wasn't something she could think about right now. She jerked the handle of her door, and opened it, jumping out, closing it behind her.

Ezra met her at the front of the pickup.

"It's up to you, but if we stay here for more than an hour or two, we're not going to be able to get married today. The courthouse closes at five, and they won't marry us after four."

"I don't think this will take long at all," she said. Definitely not an hour. And for sure not two. She would be lucky if she didn't get kicked out on her ear, but she didn't say that to Ezra. Instead, she took a deep breath, and said a small prayer.

Lord, give me courage.

She wanted to pray that her words would be accepted, that her apology would be sincere and the person she spoke to would understand that, but she didn't pray for herself, and didn't have the words to pray for her adversary. Or, the person who hopefully after today would no longer be her adversary.

She walked to the door and knocked. She could hear a child crying, someone yelling, and what sounded like a crash.

If Ezra heard, he didn't comment from behind her. She could feel his presence, but he wasn't close, respecting her wishes, and she had to remember to thank him.

After waiting for a while, she lifted her hand and knocked again, unsure as to whether or not the doorbell worked, or if they could hear over all the noise that came from inside.

Finally, she knocked a third time, wondering if all of her anxiety was for naught .If no one answered the door, she could hardly confront her past and apologize the way she needed to.

"All right, I'm coming," a woman yelled and the door jerked open. Her eyes grew big. "You!" she said.

"Shanna. I needed to apologize."

The words tumbled out, even though it probably wasn't the best way to start the conversation, but maybe she just needed to make sure that she got the words out that she needed to say, since Shanna looked like she was about ready to slam the door in her face.

"What?"

"I'm sorry."

"I don't believe you."

"It's true. I didn't know that Chalmer was married. He didn't tell me, and when I finally did find out, he told me he was leaving you. He told me that for about a year, before I finally broke up with him. But obviously, I should have walked away from him the second I knew that he had lied to me about the fact that he was married to begin with."

"I don't believe you at all. Didn't it ever seem strange to you that he never took you back to his house? Didn't you wonder where he lived? This is a small town. Everyone knows that Chalmer and I were together. We were the picture-perfect storybook couple. Until you lured him away."

She swallowed, feeling worse than she ever had in her life before. She never wanted to be the "other woman" again. She hadn't wanted to be the "other woman" to begin with.

"I'm sorry. I'm not from around here. I didn't know it. I mean, Rockerton, where I grew up, is far enough away that... I just didn't know." It was the truth. She didn't know. She might have heard of Chalmer, but her school was bigger than Sweet Water, and they never played each other. She'd had no idea that Chalmer was some kind of big shot football player in Sweet Water. Rockerton had their own big shot football players, and Alaska had made her share of mistakes, but she had steered clear of any guy who seemed like a player.

"It's too late now. The damage is done. My marriage is trash."

"I'm sorry for my part in that. I truly, truly am. Is there something I can do to make it up to you?" She hadn't intended to say that last, but an apology would be more sincere if it was accompanied by an attempt to try to make things right, even if that wasn't entirely possible.

"What are you going to do?" Shanna asked, her face clearly saying that there was nothing that she could do.

There was a crash, and then a cry, and then screaming.

Shanna looked over her shoulder and yelled, "Shut up! Or I'll give you something to cry about!"

Alaska tried not to cringe. Her mother had said that to her more than once, and she'd often wondered what it would have been like if her mother had just gone to her and put her arm around her and held her while she cried. That was the kind of mother she wanted to be.

Ezra had painted such a beautiful picture of the relationship that his parents had. He hadn't said, but she pictured his parents as being loving and kind, benevolent to their children, although Alaska was pretty sure that they had been disciplined too.

She wanted to talk to him more about it. He could tell stories about his childhood forever and she would never grow tired of listening, dreaming, wishing it had been her that had grown up in a house like that, and longing with every fiber of her being to provide a home like that for her children.

"I can't think of a thing that you can do." Shanna looked over Alaska's shoulder. "What's Ezra doing with you?"

It surprised Alaska for a moment that Shanna knew his name, but then she realized it was a small town, and Shanna probably knew everyone. That was the kind of person Shanna was. Maybe before she had children, before she'd been cheated on by her husband and divorced and thrown away like trash, maybe she'd been happy. Bubbly. Friendly, and someone who talked to everyone, who was everybody's friend.

Alaska wasn't sure, but she could picture Shanna that way.

She almost expected Ezra to say something. After all, Shanna was looking at him like she expected him to speak. But he respected what Alaska had asked, and he remained silent.

"We're on our way to get married," she finally said.

"Oh really?" Shanna batted her eyes. "Well then maybe that would be just desserts. You share your husband, the way you expected me to share mine. I would say that would be good payback."

"I'm sorry. But no." She wasn't sure whether Shanna was sincere or not. She figured that she most likely wasn't, but she didn't want to take any chances. She had heard, whether it was true or not she did not know, but she had heard that Shanna had cheated on Chalmer just as much as Chalmer had cheated on Shanna.

It didn't matter. It didn't make what Alaska did any less wrong.

"I just know I hurt you. I know I hurt your family. I know my actions were reprehensible, and absolutely wrong." Whether Chalmer had been married or not, she never should have slept with him. That was a huge mistake, compounded by the fact that he had lied to her, and had a wife and child, and then children, at home.

But, if Alaska had done the right thing to begin with, which was to tell Chalmer no and walk away from him before having a physical relationship, she wouldn't have this problem. So the responsibility had to be all on her shoulders, no matter what someone else's part in the matter was. If she didn't take responsibility for it, if she blamed someone else, then she couldn't grow and become better. She became a victim, rather than someone who controlled her situation, and therefore had the ability to make it better. Being a victim sometimes felt good, but it didn't make a person better. It couldn't. Since it abdicated them from taking any responsibility for their actions.

Alaska wanted to be different. She wanted to be better, and somehow she knew that the first step was admitting that she had done something wrong to begin with.

"That's really cute. Are you done?" Shanna asked, lifting her brows, and shifting all her weight to one foot, so her hip stuck out. She threw her shoulders back as well, and her eyes drifted back to Ezra. "I'm really not interested in cute little words, I want actions. So until you're willing to share your husband, I guess we really don't have anything to talk about."

"I'm sorry. I really am," Alaska said one more time. She had wanted forgiveness. To have the slate, if not wiped clean, at least erased. She thought if she apologized, Shanna would forgive her, and...maybe she had hopes that they would even become friends. That they would put this behind them, and their children, who were half siblings, could have a relationship somehow. She didn't even know how. She hadn't figured all of that out in her head, she just hoped... For more.

"All right. I heard you. I'm sorry," she mimicked. "But I'm not willing to do anything about it," she said, looking at Alaska in derision.

"I am. Just... Not that."

"What? Don't you think it feels good to share your husband? Do you think I wanted to?"

"I told you, I didn't think Chalmer was married. I didn't know. If I had realized when I met Chalmer that he had a wife, there wouldn't have been a relationship." She was sure about that, even though she couldn't defend herself when she found out that Chalmer had a wife and she hadn't left him. Not like they had been a couple or anything, he just came to her when he wanted... Something. He'd used her for a while, and she'd gone along with that too. Where they both got a cut from the men he found, and she'd been with. Looking back, it seemed so disgusting, but at the time, she'd needed the money.

"All right. Whatever. Just remember, when you're ready to really apologize, you know what I want." She looked at Ezra. "You're not good enough for him anyway. Look at you. Anyone who sees the two of you together will know that you did something to entice him. And we all know where you learn those things," she said. "Starting with my husband, but he wasn't the only one. There were a lot of others from what I understand. You made him a good bit of money." She wrinkled her nose at Alaska, then gave Ezra a sultry smile before she backed away and slammed the door shut, one child clinging to her leg, screaming still going on in the background.

Alaska stared at the closed door for a few minutes. That was not what she expected. She thought if she did the right thing, then good things would happen from it. She didn't think that she would get ripped up one side and down the other, and made to feel more ashamed than she had when she started.

"Are you going to try again? Or do you want to go?"

Ezra's soft words came over her shoulder.

"I can walk home from here. I just need my kids."

She didn't even know what she meant. She didn't have a home. She couldn't walk anywhere. She didn't know how she'd get her kids, and she didn't know what she was going to do. She just knew that Ezra couldn't possibly want her anymore.

"Does that mean you've changed your mind?" he asked, and she thought she detected some hurt in his voice.

She turned to look at him, and he looked concerned, upset.

"No. That means I assumed you changed yours."

"No." His jaw jutted out, although there was a muscle that ticked below his ear, and she wasn't quite sure what that meant.

"After what you just heard, are you sure?"

"I heard you trying to apologize. I saw you wanting to do the right thing. I understand that wasn't easy, and you did it anyway. I heard and saw and realized that you tried to change your life, turning from your sin, and turning to Jesus, and I know that was hard, I felt the pain of your remorse, more than I ever have in my entire life. I admired you. It was a beautiful thing to see."

She couldn't believe it. He saw good in that?

"Did you not hear what she said?"

A little smile tilted up one side of his mouth, and she could hardly believe he could find anything funny.

"I heard she seemed to get a kick out of the idea of wanting your husband, but that's me. Didn't she understand that?"

"Ezra. How could anyone look at you and not want you?" Surely he didn't actually believe that.

"Someone like Shanna? No. I don't believe for one second. I found it funny. But, you were having a hard time, and while I felt humor, I felt more anger."

"But there's no point in getting angry."

"No. There's no point in getting angry. And no point in beating a dead horse. You did what you needed to do, which was apologize. If she doesn't choose to accept it, that's on her."

"Really?" she sighed. "I don't feel any better. I wanted forgiveness. I wanted her to say... Maybe not that's okay, but I wanted her to make me feel like what I did wasn't hurting her still. That we had a clean slate between us. I think some weird part of me also thought that maybe we could be friends, that our children would grow up together, considering that they have the same father."

"I want to be the father of your children."

"I can't believe it."

"I don't understand why not. I've been saying the same thing over and over. I don't typically say things I don't mean."

"I'm not used to that either, but it just seems so...crazy. Like if you told me that you could fly, and that you were going to the moon, that's how crazy it sounds."

"Well, I have no desire to leave North Dakota. I love it here. And I hope to stay. Forever. I even have my grave plot picked out."

"Don't talk like that!" She couldn't even think about graves and dying. Ezra was the one solid thing in her life right now, and if he still wanted her, she would happily go with him. She couldn't bear the idea that anything could happen to him, and that the one really great thing in her life could get knocked out from underneath her.

Except, he wasn't the one great thing in her life. That was God.

"I think she likes me," he said, and then smiled that half smile he did, the one that made her heart flip over.

"I do. You said something yesterday about the more you talk to me the more you wanted to talk to me, or something like that."

"It's true. The more time I spend with you, the more I want to spend."

"That's happening to me. You were here, I mean, you didn't say anything, and I appreciated that, and maybe that was part of it. You just... Were there for me. And you did what I asked you to do, and you didn't fight with me or argue or tell me how I was doing it wrong, you just... Supported me however you could, and it made me feel like it didn't matter if I failed, you were still going to be there for me."

"It's true. I will. That's part of what being married is. You're there for the other person, not as a judge, not as a mother, or a commander, but as a companion, as a support. Someone to stand beside you, not over you or to browbeat you."

"That feels so good. I... I've never had that in my life before. If that's what being married is like, I can't wait."

"Speaking of, we can go?"

"Yeah. It makes me sad. That didn't end the way I hoped it would."

"I'm sure. But that's not your fault. Your apology was sincere, and you were humble and contrite. Shanna didn't want to accept your apology. I think sometimes when someone is coming to you humbly, you feel like you can lord it over them, and when you don't have character, that's what you do. Instead of accepting their apology, you rub in how wrong they were. And try to make them feel as bad as you can. I don't know why that makes some people feel powerful, but it does."

"Maybe that's why apologizing is so hard. You give the other person the opportunity to do that. Sometimes they take it."

"I think more times than what we want to admit, they take it. After all, apologizing wouldn't be difficult if we weren't afraid that people were going to treat us the way Shanna just treated you."

"I guess the thing that I can learn from that is that I don't want to treat other people the way that she treated me just now. So I'll have to try to remember that when someone apologizes, even if I don't want to forgive, I want to have the character to not be unkind at the very least."

"Exactly."

His hand came up, touched her shoulder, and then slid around to her back.

"Is this okay?" he asked.

He was so...considerate. So concerned about her. He treated her with far more deference than what she deserved. Although maybe if he understood everything she'd done, he wouldn't be so concerned about asking if his hand on her back was okay. She'd certainly allowed far more with far less pleasure.

"I like it," she said sincerely.

Her words made him smile, and he pulled her to him. She went willingly, remembering what he had said about wanting her to touch him. She put her arm around his waist, and they walked back to his pickup together, with him walking to her side, and opening her door for her.

He seemed too good to be true. A man who asked her before he touched her. Who opened her door for her. Who stood beside her. She didn't deserve all of this.

Lord? Is this some kind of trick you're playing on me? What's the punchline? I keep waiting for it. I know it can't be for real.

But, as he helped her in the truck and closed the door behind her, she knew that he was very, very real. And that this was a dangerous place for her to be. Because she was tempted to trust him, and in her experience, trusting a man only led to pain and suffering.

Part of her really, really wanted to. Saying that Ezra was different than any man she knew, which was true.

And in that case, it made her want to be better, someone who deserved a man like Ezra.

Chapter Seventeen

Alaska had been quiet since she talked to Shanna. Ezra thought it was mostly because things hadn't gone the way she wanted them to, but he also wondered if there might be a little bit more to it than that. She kept saying things like she didn't deserve him, or that she couldn't believe him, and he didn't know what to do about it.

He didn't exactly want to tell her all the terrible things he had ever done, but he wasn't nearly as perfect as she seemed to think he was.

Talking to her earlier had really seemed to help, and, while he wasn't exactly a let's all talk about our emotions kind of person, maybe he needed to become more like that for his wife. He truly did want a relationship like his parents, although, he didn't want to put pressure on Alaska to be something that she wasn't, or to feel like she had to be different than what she was.

He didn't know how to tell her all of that, to let her know that he wanted them to have a relationship that worked for both of them, and not necessarily a carbon copy of his parents, but they could still use his parents as an example, right? It seemed like they had a very biblical relationship, but they also had...more. Affection and respect between them.

Still, she seemed down, and he wasn't sure what to do. When he asked her if she wanted to eat out, she declined, saying they ought to get back to the kids.

Maybe he could start there.

"So, we talked a little bit about the kids," he started, hoping that she would respond, and be willing to talk to him.

"Yeah? Is there something you wanted to say?" she asked, fingering the band that he put on her finger. It had been his mother's. He hadn't asked her about it, because he was afraid she would decline. It actually meant a lot to him to have her wear it, and he didn't want to take a chance that she would say no. He supposed that was the coward's way out.

"Yes, I guess. I just wanted to make sure that…we're on the same page. I don't know what it takes to adopt them, and maybe you don't want me to do that."

"I'd really like it if you would."

"Maybe I can get the same attorney that I got when we needed the PFA."

"I didn't realize you had to go through an attorney."

"I figured it would be best. It's in place, by the way."

"Oh. That's good."

"He's out," Ezra said, realizing he probably should have told her what his attorney had messaged him earlier when he was out fixing the water trough. He supposed the idea of getting married and all the other things that had been happening had gotten in the way.

"You mean Rex?"

"Yeah."

"I hope after that he's not going to be much of a problem. He obviously didn't get what he wanted the last time."

"You don't think he'll try again?"

"I want to think that he wouldn't, but… Maybe he will."

"I think that we ought to assume that he would, and make a plan. But, that really wasn't what I was thinking with the kids, although we should have a plan for them as well."

"All right. I don't really know anything about that, other than I've seen people do some pretty terrible things in the name of drugs and money."

"That's too bad. But that's the world we live in. And I think we ought to be ready, rather than taken by surprise. Even if nothing ever happens."

"I guess I can't argue with that."

"But the kids. I... I assume that both of us would be raising them. That we would talk about things, and that you would really want me to be the dad. I don't want to step on your toes, if that's not what you had in mind. But, that's what I would like. They are going to be in my house, I want to be a parent who is involved." He wanted to be involved in loving them, disciplining them, playing with them, just making them a family.

"That's what I would like. I guess I don't know a whole lot about raising children, and you watched your parents raise twelve kids, and they all seem to have turned out okay. Whereas for me, I had a terrible example, and I haven't exactly turned out well."

"I think you turned out really well. Especially after I watched what you did today. I'm telling you, it's uncommon, and I thought it was beautiful."

"I know you said that. I guess it's just hard for me to believe. I want to though."

"Keep working on it until you do. Because I mean it, and I'm not going to change my mind about that or about anything else."

"You keep saying that, but you don't understand, you haven't seen, you just don't know —"

"I don't have to. When you say that you're going to do something, it shouldn't depend on circumstances. I suppose there are times where you can't do what you say you're going to do because circumstances change, but when you're loyal to someone, it doesn't matter what they do. When you make vows to someone, it doesn't matter what they do."

"That's a code of conduct I'm just not familiar with."

He kept his eyes on the road, driving in North Dakota wasn't hard. It was mostly straight, the roads were wide, even if they were a little rough because of the difficult winters and all the freezing and thawing that happened. Still, because of the straightness of the roads, sometimes it was easy for a person to get complacent, and to not pay attention. He didn't want to get so wrapped up in the conversation that he forgot to drive. Not that he ever had that problem before, but Alaska was different.

"Well, I can't say that I'm perfect. I had the feeling earlier that you seemed to think I am, and maybe we can talk later. But, I'm not. You saw what a mess I made with Sondra. That's because of me. Not because of her."

"I would lay some of the blame at Sondra's feet," Alaska said, and there was humor in her voice.

He chuckled, but he didn't agree. He could have headed that off back when it first started, if he'd only opened his mouth and said something that would have been a little bit difficult, but true. Instead, he took the easy road.

"That's an example of how sometimes we don't do the hard thing that we know we should, and it ends up complicating things even worse."

"I've done that a lot in my life."

"A lot of times the hard road is something we avoid, but usually we don't regret taking it."

"I agree"

"Anyway, that's off the subject. I mean, we can talk about it if we want to, but I just wanted to make sure that when I'm saying 'our' kids, it's not something that bothers you. Because I want to think of them as ours."

"No. It actually makes me feel good. Like you truly do care about them and are interested in us."

"I am."

"That makes me happy. But it increases that feeling of feeling like... like God is playing some kind of weird trick on me. I don't want to wake up and find out this is all some kind of dream, because that's what it feels like. Too good to be true."

"We're going to have hard times. Things aren't always going to be easy. And, I think we as humans have a tendency to get used to things, and they don't feel so special anymore."

"You don't think this will always feel special to me?"

He shook his head. He was almost certain of it. Things that were new and exciting eventually lost their glow, and then they just felt normal, and humans had a tendency to continuously go after the things that made them feel fresh and exciting, rather than sticking with the same old same old.

"Maybe that's one reason to try to keep affection and respect in our marriage, the way my parents did. Not that I want to hold them up as some kind of goal for us. Just... I think they were onto something when they made sure that they were careful with each other. That they treated their relationship as precious."

"I think you're right. I'd really like to try to do that, and from where I'm sitting right now, it seems like an easy thing, but I suppose most people start out thinking that it will be easy, and then... It doesn't happen."

"No. People get angry, they get annoyed, they start thinking that they made a mistake, that the things that are wrong with their spouse are too hard to accept, or that they could find a better person somewhere else and they start looking around. I think that's partly what dating does to our culture."

"Dating? You think there's something wrong with dating?"

"I figure that it's just practice for divorce. After all, we check out this person, are with them for a while, tire of them, and then we go to someone else. They're the next best thing, until we decide we don't really want to be with them anymore either, and we see someone else who catches our eye and that's totally acceptable. I mean, our culture even encourages it. 'You should stay with someone who makes you happy.' That type of thing. But that's the exact opposite of what marriage is supposed to be. So we're not really practicing to get married, we're practicing to get divorced when we date."

Maybe he should have just kept his mouth shut. He had some really odd ideas, things that went against what everyone else in the world believed, even Christians. And, he obviously shocked Alaska.

"Maybe you're not going to want me to help you raise your kids after all, if I'm not going to want them to date." He said that with a smile, but there was a seriousness behind his words that she seemed to catch.

"No. What you said just made sense, although I've never taken the time to think about it. I can't really think of any argument to present to you to make it sound like you're wrong. Because... The only thing I can think of is how are you going to find the person that you want to marry? But here I am, sitting beside someone I never dated in my life, and I'm married to him."

"It's kind of funny how God works if we let Him, isn't it?" he said, with a lifting of his lips.

"So you think that all of these terrible things that happened to me was God working?"

"Do you think it wasn't?" She sat there for a moment, processing. Then she said,

"God is good. Could He let all those bad things in my life? Do you really want me to believe that God was behind that terrible stuff?"

"No. But maybe He allowed it so that it would work for His purpose. You have to admit, we wouldn't be sitting here today if you hadn't been through what you were, right?"

"I suppose. But, you know it would be so much nicer if you could see the end as you are going through all the hard things. I spent a lot of days depressed and despondent and only chose to live because of my kids."

That made him sad, and a little scared. "You know, God has a purpose for you."

"What? To make *you* a better person? Because you have to put up with me all the time, for a lifetime now?"

"No. Hardly. Maybe you'll make me a better person, but not because I have to put up with you. Because you inspire me. Like you did today. And, you make me laugh. Like you do all the time. I'm sure we'll find other things as well." He thought about the idea of having someone beside him now. Someone who looked at him and saw good. A good man. Who admired him. Would she grow to see his flaws? Would they become bigger in her eyes? Would the glow of admiration dim?

He hoped not. He supposed it wasn't really his job to keep it there, although he wanted to be the kind of man she could admire and respect. Who she enjoyed being with.

They rode on in silence, maybe both of them lost in their thoughts, until he pulled up beside the house. It was starting to get dark, although the big house was brightly lit and there was a light on in the small house in the kitchen.

"Can we just walk around?" he asked, not wanting to deal with his siblings after everything that they had gone through that day.

"Sure. Are you ashamed of me?" she asked, and while the question was said lightly, he suppose there was more truth in it than she wanted to admit.

"No. I'm not. Actually, let's walk through. I bet they're eating."

Sure enough, when they walked in, he could hear his siblings in the kitchen, silverware clanking, as they talked and laughed together.

Alaska seemed to hold back as they stepped in, and he tugged on her hand. "Are you okay?"

"This is so foreign." She took a steadying breath.

"It's your new normal," he said, meeting her eyes, and wishing that he could impose upon her the confidence that her life was what she made of it. And this could be hers, if she made it that way.

But he understood even though he'd grown up in a home exactly like this, he didn't always know how to go about getting it.

Chapter Eighteen

"Hey, there's the happy couple," Caleb said as they walked in. Caleb was always the first one to have something to say.

"Congratulations you two," Phoebe said smiling. She pushed back away from the table and got up and came over and gave Alaska a hug.

Ezra made a mental note to thank her later. Priscilla and Ada pushed in, until all three of them were hugging Alaska. He thought Alaska probably was a little overwhelmed, but he didn't ask his sisters to stand back. He wanted her to know that they welcomed her.

"Welcome to the family," Tobias said, with his hand out once the girls moved away.

Alaska looked at it, and then took it carefully.

"I think she thinks you're going to hurt her, bro. Stop looking so... Scary," Caleb joked as he held his own hand out for Alaska. "Welcome, kiddo."

It was the kiddo that reminded Ezra that Alaska was so much younger than he was. He had a tendency to completely forget. He wasn't sure their age mattered, really. She probably lived more lifetimes than he ever would, had more experiences, and new things that he would never know, not unless she told him. And he wondered if she ever would. There were some things a person just couldn't talk about.

He hoped Alaska felt like she could talk to him though.

"How did it go? Did they let you marry him even though he has a criminal record" Caleb said, smacking Ezra on the back.

"What?" Alaska looked confused.

"He's messing with you." Ezra said, smacking Caleb back, perhaps a little harder than necessary.

"It sounded good, anyway," Caleb said with a grin.

"It didn't sound the slightest bit believable to me," Alaska said. Ezra appreciated the fact that she was defending him. Even if it was against his own siblings. Or maybe especially. It would be easy to be drawn into their banter, but she was letting them know that she stood firmly beside him. He put a hand on her shoulder, and drew her carefully to him, and was cheered when she allowed him to do so, slipping her own arm around his waist again as she had done earlier that day.

He thought maybe they were building something that would last a lifetime. He hoped so.

"We just wanted to stop in and say hi. We're headed back over to the little house."

"You can eat here if you want to," Priscilla offered.

"I think the kids are probably over there, and we should get back and let Nelda have a break. The poor lady."

"Yeah. Poor lady, doing exactly what she loves to do. You've made her day." Caleb walked back over to the table and sat down. There wasn't too much that got between him and his food.

"You know, you could make her day, and get married and have some children of your own," Ezra said.

"I guess when God drops a woman into my lap like he dropped one into yours, I'll let you know. Also, by the way, there was no suspicious activity around the ranch today, just in case you were wondering."

"I do appreciate you keeping an eye out for that. Thanks. We got a PFA in place, although he's out of jail."

"We'll continue to keep an eye out for things, listen for the dogs barking. You know, maybe you'd want to take one over to your house."

"I guess we could. How do you feel about that? Anyone allergic?" He looked down at Alaska, who seemed to appreciate the fact that he was standing beside her. He knew his family could be a little overwhelming, with all of the people and the noise and the way conversations went back and forth from subject to subject.

He had been told that by his friends at times, although most of them grew to love being included in all the hubbub.

"No. Not that I know of. And I think the kids would really love it."

"Want to take Barney? He is a good one."

Barney was some kind of mix they'd picked up along the road about a decade before. They had no idea how old he was when they got him, but he'd been a good dog, loyal and protective, and patient. With the children, that might be the key.

At the sound of his name, Barney padded into the kitchen.

"I guess he wants to go," Ezra said, looking at the dog who had stopped beside him and looked up with soulful eyes. "Is Barney okay with you?" He needed to remember that it wasn't just him anymore. Of course, it had always been his siblings and him, but now he needed to make sure that he checked with his wife before he made any serious decisions.

"Sure. That's fine. He looks like a real sweetheart. Has he ever been around children?" Alaska asked, as she knelt to pet Barney. He allowed it, and put his nose on her cheek.

It seemed to charm her, because she smiled and gave him a hug.

"Yeah. He was around mine, and they love him." Priscilla sounded a little sad. Of course.

No one else said anything, and the room was quiet for a bit.

Ezra figured Alaska probably wondered what was going on, and he thought that maybe he'd have to tell her a little bit about Priscilla's background, and her nasty divorce. But, maybe not today.

It might be something that Priscilla would want to tell herself.

They moved through the kitchen, going out the back door, and down the steps.

"We probably ought to make some kind of driveway that stops at our house, so we don't have to walk through the farmhouse to get to ours." Ezra spoke as he mentally put that on his list. When they bought the place, it hadn't been a big deal, but now that it was going to be his private residence, he figured Alaska would want a little privacy from his family.

"I can't believe there wasn't one."

"There might have been at one time. I'm sure the original farmhouse was where the kids grew up, and then probably someone wanted to get married, or else the parents wanted to retire. Whatever it was, someone moved out of the big farmhouse into the little one, and I'm guessing they had their own driveway and all of that. But, as years went by, whoever bought it didn't use the little house. For whatever reason. And it just grew over. But, I think there may be a fence or two that we'll have to move if we want to get enough room so that we can turn around comfortably."

"I don't want to be a major imposition. I... I'm fine with it the way it is."

"You might be fine, but you deserve to have a little bit of privacy, and you certainly deserve your own driveway. Don't worry about putting people out. That's what life is about. You do things for others, and that means that you can't do something for yourself, and that's okay. That's life. And, as Christians, we want to do that. We shouldn't want to spend all of our free time on ourselves."

"You've said that before, but you're right. I just... I'm not used to it. Where I come from, everybody is pretty much out for themselves. It's unusual to find anyone who will do something for you without payment, or some kind of compensation. You scratch my back, I'll scratch yours, so to speak."

"Yeah. That's kind of the way people want to be, but Jesus teaches us something completely different. It's a harder thing to do, but it's much more rewarding."

"I have to agree with you."

They had reached the steps and started up them.

"I had meant to ask you earlier. Should... Should the kids call me dad? I mean, I don't want to —"

"Yes! I'm so glad you said something. Absolutely. Um..." she stopped in front of the door, and he stopped beside her. Something about her posture made him look down, wondering what it was.

"I don't have a father's name on the birth certificate. I... I always assumed they were Chalmers, but...there's a chance they're not."

That was hard. As hard as it was to listen to her today in front of

Shanna, when she was talking about the things that she had done with Chalmer for money. He didn't want to think about it. Not just because of what she had done, but because of how it had to have affected her. She was trying to live right, she couldn't be proud of those moments, and... He guessed that they were a lot more painful than she let on.

"I'm sorry," was the only thing he could think of to say.

"I should have told you that before we got married. I... I know you heard me talking to Shanna —"

"I did. And I felt bad for you."

"Isn't there anything I could do that would make you turn away from me?" she asked, and she sounded frustrated. Like she had been trying to upset him.

"Am I not reacting the way you want me to?" he asked, and his voice was gentle, although there was a little bit of...fear. Fear that she was trying to push him away. He didn't know what he would do about that.

"No! You're not reacting the way I expect you to! I expect you to be horrified, disgusted, appalled. Not...compassionate and forgiving."

"There's nothing that I need to forgive you for. As for being compassionate, I think that's the natural response. You had a hard life. You had to do things you didn't want to do."

"That's just it! At the time, I did want to do those things. At least, I wanted the money from doing those things, and it didn't seem like a big deal. Like I was just doing business."

"You had to do things you regret." He corrected himself.

She nodded. "You're right. I do regret them. I have a lot of regrets."

"You know, when God forgives you, He forgives everything. He doesn't remember. That's what He wants for you and me. I have to forgive you, and you forgive me. And we're supposed to do it the way God forgives us. Of anything." He paused, because his heart really did hurt with a sadness and pain that was totally unfamiliar. "I'm not saying it's easy."

"No. And we don't deserve forgiveness," she said, almost as though she had finally figured out what was going on. Why he was forgiving, and why she couldn't do anything that would make him turn his back on her.

"Because there's nothing that we can do that would make God turn his back on us."

"Yeah. I just figured it all out."

"That doesn't mean it doesn't hurt." He figured he ought to say that, because it was true. It was painful. "I suppose that's true for the Lord too. It hurts Him when we sin."

"That makes me sad. I had never even thought about that before. But the same way that our sin hurts people around us, it hurts God, too."

"The way a child's sin hurts their parents. You want the best for your kid, you want them to do right, and when they don't, it's hard. Painful. And that's the way God feels about us and our sin when we sin."

"I've never seen that before, but it's so clear now."

They stood there staring at each other, maybe thinking a little, and he finally said, "It's been a long day. Come on. Let's go and see our kids."

"Our kids," she echoed. Then he smiled. He didn't know what it was going to take to adopt them, but he wanted to. He wanted them to be a family and he was going to put every single effort that he possibly could into making that happen. Not just because he wanted to, but because that's what happened when God forgave them. They got adopted into God's family, and treated like one of God's own. It almost seemed like that was the example that Ezra had, and it was the one that he was supposed to follow. He was going to do it to the best of his ability.

Chapter Nineteen

"And every time it rains, God puts his rainbow in the sky to remind us that he will never flood the earth with water again."

Alaska closed the Bible story book she had been reading and stroked with a gentle hand across Eugene's forehead.

"I'll see you in the morning, okay?"

Eugene nodded sleepily as he pulled his blanket a little further up around his chin.

Alice was already in her crib, and although she wasn't asleep, she lay on her mattress with sleepy eyes turned toward her mom.

Bedtime did not always go this quietly or easily, but Alaska was glad tonight had been one of the better nights. Ezra sat at the foot of Eugene's bed, watching and listening.

When she stood, putting the story book on top of his dresser, and tiptoeing out of the room, Ezra followed.

Today had gone so much better than she had expected. Ezra was... More. Even though, he had been trying to convince her that he wasn't perfect, and she believed him, of course, he was so much more than what she deserved. He had been better to her already in just one day than she could ever remember any man being to her in her life before.

It had been quite an eventful day, and she was exhausted. But, there was one married thing that she knew she could do really well, and, if the truth be told, she'd been looking forward to it.

She closed the door quietly with a soft click, and then stood in front of it. Ezra had stopped in the hall and turned around and looked at her standing in the soft glow of the single bathroom in the house. He kept calling it the little house, and it was small, with only two bedrooms and one bath, with a kitchen and living room downstairs, but it was bigger than a lot of the places she'd been.

"That was beautiful. Do you do that every night?" Ezra said softly as she stood, waiting for him to lead the way to their bedroom.

"It doesn't always go that well, but yeah. I try to read a story as often as I can. Maybe five nights out of seven. But I just see bedtime as an opportunity to... Not connect with my kids, exactly, but at least spend a little time together where we're winding down our day and it makes good memories."

"There were so many kids in our house, our parents never really had a bedtime routine where they spent individual time with each of us. It was more of an 'okay it's time to go to bed, brush your teeth, change your clothes and get in bed' and that was it."

Was he saying that she was actually doing something better than his family?

"You always hold your family up as an example. I'm sometimes a little jealous, and a lot intimidated. I appreciate you letting me know that maybe I'm doing something right."

"I don't have to talk about them if you don't want me to." He said that immediately, and sincerely, and she believed him, but she didn't want to stop talking about his family.

"That's part of your past. It's a good part. It works. I mean, twelve kids might be a little much, but..."

"How many kids is the right amount?" he asked, and she supposed every married couple had to have this conversation, but maybe they usually had it before they got married.

"I don't know. Sometimes I can hardly handle two. I can't imagine more."

"My mom had six or eight I think before Nelda started helping us. After that, I think things got easier, but raising children is not an easy job. It's exhausting, and it never ends. It's not like you get the weekends off."

"Yeah. Or any day off. Although you're right, having Nelda watch them was really nice. We had the whole day and I didn't hardly have to worry about them. Although I did... When you said that he was out of jail —"

"Yeah. I should have told you I texted my brothers and let them know that they needed to be extra vigilant. We're going to try hard not to let what happened before, happen again."

"Thank you. I do worry about that a little bit. Not for me. For my kids."

"Well I'm concerned for all of you, but I don't want to call it worry. Worry is a sin, but it's wise to be prepared, and sometimes worry does that to us. It helps us be prepared." He hooked a hand around the back of his neck, and shifted from one foot to the other.

Alaska smiled at his obvious unease. This was one area where she had more experience than he did, and perhaps even more confidence. It wasn't necessarily a good thing, and it wasn't that she was proud of her past. But, good things could happen out of bad things, and she might as well take her experience and her confidence and put them to use for her husband. She stepped forward two steps before placing a hand on Ezra's chest. The man jumped. And she hid a smile.

"I think it's bedtime for us," she said softly, looking up, and knowing that the smile on her face was as old as Eve.

Ezra stared down at her, the dim light in the hall making it difficult to read his eyes since his face was cast in shadow. She could tell his mouth was unsmiling.

His hand came up and covered hers, but it didn't press it closer. His fingers wrapped around hers and pulled them away from his chest. Their hands fell between them, although he didn't let go. She saw it as a rejection, and a little part of her withered. Did he not want her?

"I think I better sleep on the couch tonight," Ezra said and while there was a bit of sadness in his words, there was something else, too. Something that made his breath hitch and his words sound...almost breathless.

"You don't have to. Not for me. This is one area where I really do think that I might not have everything down, but I'm good at."

He laughed, but there wasn't much humor in it. "It's probably the opposite for me. I'm definitely not confident. But, I do think we probably ought to know each other a little better, as much as I would... be okay with not. Just...it seems to be wiser to have a better foundation between the two of us before we move into something physical."

She blinked a little, because while she'd heard various places that a physical relationship wasn't the best way to start a marriage, it was definitely part of the relationship between a man and a woman, and they were married, so it was okay.

"If you're doing it for me, you don't have to. I'm ready." She paused. "And willing." She wasn't sure if she should have added that last. Or maybe she should have said eager. That was true. There was just something about Ezra that made her feel like he was going to take care of her no matter what. She felt like she could trust him. Even though she hadn't known him that long. She just knew that he wasn't going to do anything that was going to hurt her. Not on purpose anyway.

"Maybe you're not as ready as what you think." His words were soft, and a little sad still.

"Maybe I am. I mean, I probably know myself better than anyone, right?"

He swallowed. The sound seemed to echo in the hall, like his throat was tight and it was hard to get it to work.

"Maybe I'm just being afraid. But I like to think it's more that I'm being noble. Is that arrogant?"

"I don't think so, but I don't think it's necessary either." She didn't want to push them into doing something that he didn't want to do, but she also didn't want to not give this part of their marriage attention. Not only was it her strongest area, but a physical relationship between a man and woman was just as important as whatever kind of relationship he was talking about as a foundation. At least in her opinion. Of course, she wouldn't argue that it should be the first thing, but once a couple was married, there was no reason not to develop that relationship too.

"Do what you want," she said, surprised at how easily the words came out. She wanted Ezra to be the head of their home. That was the biblical mandate, that the man was the head. She wanted to do what God wanted. But, she also really wanted her way with this. She felt like it was important. "I will try not to talk you into this, but I don't think there's any need for you to sleep on the couch."

His fingers tightened around hers, and she squeezed back.

"I can't deny it's tempting," Ezra said, and there was a wobble in his voice. It wasn't nearly as confident as it usually was, and she didn't know how to fix it.

He didn't move to come any closer, or to turn toward the bedroom. He just stood there, like he was thinking, or maybe like he couldn't make a decision.

"This is one temptation you don't have to try to resist. And, I've been thinking a lot about it today, looking forward to it." Surely he had too?

"I decided that wasn't going to happen tonight. I decided that I was going to sleep on the couch before I even woke up this morning. It was a decision I made when we agreed to get married yesterday."

"Why?"

"Because. We barely know each other. And, I think... I think it will be more meaningful if we have a solid friendship."

"And maybe sleeping together will help us get to know each other faster."

A muscle ticked in his jaw as he stared at her. Finally he said, "I can't think of any good argument. I just have a gut feeling. Don't you feel it too?" He looked away, over her head at the back wall, almost as though he were trying to marshal his thoughts. "I mean, I feel pulled toward you. I told you I want to, it's not a matter of me not wanting." He looked down, his eyes a little wide like he was concerned that she might have taken his reluctance that way.

"I did wonder," she murmured.

"Yeah. Don't." His free hand came up, and his fingers brushed softly over her hairline, down her cheek, and his eyes watched, almost as though he couldn't believe his fingers were touching her. "You're so soft. So...beautiful."

She shook her head a little. "Not beautiful."

"You are to me." It was all Ezra said. It was like he wasn't going to try to talk her into believing anyone else thought that, but she couldn't deny that he would speak the truth to her.

She contemplated that as she looked up to him. There hadn't been a lot of people who had called her beautiful in her life. At least not with some kind of ulterior motive. Most of the time, the men she'd been with, hadn't needed to. There had been already an understanding about what was going to happen, and they didn't need to be tender or gentle. The way Ezra was being as his fingers trailed down her neck and moved under her hair.

"I think I can spend a lot of time touching, and not need to do anything else. You...feel a lot different than I do."

"I think that's the point, isn't it? I'm supposed to feel different."

"Better. You feel better. Softer. More delicate. And yeah, I guess you're right.That's the attraction right there. You're different. Better."

"Not better. Because, I don't really want you to feel soft, or delicate." There was humor in her eyes as she looked up at him, but he didn't really smile back.

"That's a good thing. You'd be disappointed."

It felt to her like he might have been saying more than his words would indicate. Like he wasn't just talking about how he felt, but more. She didn't know how to reassure him. And she had to admit it made her feel a little powerful, to think that someone who was as confident as Ezra, would be... insecure because of her.

"I'm not going to be disappointed. Promise."

"Normally, if I'm not sure about something, I'd do some research on it. Look it up on the internet. But I'm pretty sure it's not a good idea to research 'how to not disappoint your wife.'"

"And I told you, you don't have to worry about it."

"I'm afraid you might be wrong about that," he said.

She stepped closer, and ran her fingers lightly up his back over his T-shirt. "I guess you'll just have to trust me on this. But I can tell you, it doesn't matter what you do, or what you don't do, or anything in between. Maybe it's what you were saying. About having a connection outside of the physical. I already feel like...maybe we don't know each other as well as we could, but that I can trust you. I think that's probably the key. I feel like whatever happens, you're going to put me ahead of yourself. It's just the way you are. And... I think that's what makes for good intimacy. When you have trust, and you know that the other person is not out to be selfish and greedy, but is about you. You're more concerned about me. That... Already makes me feel cherished."

His eyes narrowed a little, as though he were thinking about what she was saying. Maybe he'd never heard it put that way, or maybe he'd never really thought about it.

"I thought that's what this was. I mean, I assumed it was supposed to be good for both of us, but I thought the point was the other person."

"I've heard a lot of teaching, especially with women, that it has to be about you. That you have to make sure that it's good for yourself, and I found that's probably true when you're with someone who doesn't care about you. But, when you're with the right person," she smiled a little. "And I know I'm with the right person. Then that doesn't matter. Because the point is not to make yourself feel good. The point is to share something with someone else, and make it beautiful together."

He nodded, swallowing hard again. "I would agree with that."

"And, it's tempting for me to say that all men are the same, but I don't think that's true. Husbands are different than other men." She bit her lip. She didn't want to remind him of all the things that she'd done, but maybe because of those things, she knew that there was a difference now.

"You've never been married before."

She shook her head.

"Then this is your first time with your husband."

"Yeah. And it's already been different." Typically she didn't have anyone who wanted to stand around and talk about things. They all wanted to get to the "good stuff." But Ezra had been willing to talk about everything. Anything. All day long, even though he wasn't good at it, he seemed to know it was something she needed. To work things out, to have them in the air between them, to put them out there so her brain could process them with his input.

"Because I'm slow?" he said, and for the first time there was a bit of a smile on his face

"I'm pretty sure, in this area at least, slow is good."

"It's kind of what I thought too."

"So did I talk you out of going to the couch?" she asked, as her fingers found the small dip in his back where his backbone was, and she followed it down to the waistband of his jeans. The humor faded from his face.

"Are you sure?" he asked, like she hadn't just spent the last ten minutes trying to convince him to do what she wanted, rather than what he said he was going to do.

"I'm sure. But I don't want you to be upset with me if waiting is something that's important to you."

"I think it might be the smarter thing to do." His mouth closed, and he pressed his lips together before he said, "but, maybe... Maybe a good night kiss wouldn't be a bad idea."

It was a small victory, but she smiled anyway. "I think that would be a really great idea."

He nodded. "So, just kissing tonight. And, we'll probably need a lot of practice on that, so...the rational part of my brain wants to put a time limit on kissing. Like we should schedule how many days we'll kiss, but maybe that's not a good idea."

"No. Maybe things will just happen naturally."

"I think so. But you're okay with this?"

"I'm okay with so much more than kissing." She just reminded him, so he wouldn't forget, that if they only had a good night kiss tonight, it was because he decided, not her.

He smiled a little, a slow smile, humor and affection on his face as his hand let go of hers, and both of them went around her back, stroking down the way she'd traced down his. "I was a little worried about what you've done, and how you've done it, and then I just decided that it doesn't matter. And we're going to do this my way."

Maybe it was the control freak coming out in him. Probably being the oldest of any number of siblings made a person a little more controlling than average, but she didn't care.

"I want it to be your way. That was the point." He lowered his head, and her breath caught. She hadn't been joking when she said he'd already been different than any other man she'd ever been with. And while she regretted those memories, wished they weren't there, it was also nice in a way that she wasn't afraid.

Her hands went over his shoulders and wrapped around his neck, tugging gently, as he lowered his head.

Maybe her impatience made him smile, or maybe it was just her. But, she saw his lips were tilted up before she closed her eyes, and lifted her face to meet his.

She didn't feel fireworks or any kind of crazy thing like that, but when his lips settled over hers, she definitely had a feeling of rightness, of perfection, of total contentment, and while the flame of desire was there, the feeling of being cherished, of being appreciated for who she was, the gentleness he showed, the sweet tenderness, made any other man she'd ever kissed fade away, leaving room for only Ezra, and how perhaps his kiss wasn't the most skillful, but it was the most perfect.

Her lungs didn't want to work as he pulled away, and she dug her fingers into his shoulders to keep her balance when he lifted his head.

"That didn't really feel like good night to me," Ezra said softly.

"Me either," she said, hoping that that meant he was going to do it again. She couldn't quite figure out how he could make her feel so crazy and yet so secure at the same time. It was like being strapped into a roller coaster.

"But I think it better be." He ran a hand over her hair again, slowly, like he was thinking about the way it felt. She really liked how conscientious he was, how each thing that he did he did slowly and deliberately like he enjoyed it, and wanted to savor her. Rather than rushing, or being impatient. Maybe that was his age more than anything. She didn't care, she just liked it.

"I'm not going to say I'm not disappointed. That was the best kiss I've ever had."

He chuckled, like what she said was funny. "I definitely think I can use some practice. And if you're willing, then, I think we ought to definitely make some time every day for practicing."

"That won't be a hardship for me."

He smiled and stepped back. "It was a good day. Thank you. I... Should have spent the whole day with you. I'm sorry."

She'd forgotten that he hadn't been there that morning. And while she appreciated his apology, she figured that there probably were going to be plenty of days he had to work, since the ranch was a little different than most businesses. It didn't shut down at a certain time and the employees went home.

"I'll take whatever you give me. And I'll appreciate it."

His smile faded a little, and he said, "You deserve a lot more."

She started to shake her head, and then feeling a little crafty, she said, "Then I'll take another kiss."

He laughed then, and she felt like she scored a victory. Making Ezra laugh, because the sound wasn't common, and she cherished it.

"I can't tell the lady no. Especially when I enjoyed the first one so much." He stepped closer, and it was a good long while before she walked to her room alone.

Chapter Twenty

"Y ou've been smiling a lot today. Last night must have been pretty
good."

Ezra blinked and looked at his brother. He realized after the words penetrated his brain that Caleb was right. He was smiling an awful lot. Not for the reason that Caleb probably assumed, but because he felt like, first of all, he'd made the right decision to not push Alaska, even though she had been willing, which, that in itself made him smile.

He offered to marry her to protect her, to give her the protection of his family and his friends, but...he had felt something more for her from the beginning. Because he didn't think he would offer to marry just anyone. He had a good time with her. He definitely enjoyed kissing her. And he was hopeful. Hopeful that what they had started yesterday would stretch into a lifetime of shared laughter, shared hopes and dreams, and yes, shared passion.

"And the man has no comment on that?" Caleb said, as they unloaded the roll of woven wire from the back of the ATV.

"I think I read somewhere that you're not supposed to kiss and tell. So yeah, the man has no comment."

"I don't know. I haven't seen you smile like that since... Ever. Maybe I should go looking for a wife for myself."

"You probably should. You're not getting any younger."

"You're always going to be the old man."

"I can handle it." Although, when he thought about Alaska, and how she was only twenty-five, he did pause a little. He didn't think of her as young. Maybe he should try to remember. But she just seemed so much more mature.

He had wanted to take her with him today. But, Caleb and he were fixing fence, and he was up and out of the house before Alaska came down the stairs. Claudia had cooked breakfast, and he grabbed something from the main house before he and Caleb headed out.

"I think if I get married, I'm going to want my wife to work with me. I'm definitely not going to want to get up and have to spend the day with my brother," Caleb said conversationally as they threw off a couple fence posts. There was just a small section that had been broken down because the electric wire on the top hadn't been hot and the cows had pushed on it.

There was always something to fix, whether it was fence, a water trough, or pieces of equipment. Something was always breaking down. Part of being a rancher was being able to fix stuff. Any kind of stuff.

"So did you get a good price for the weaners?" Caleb asked as they continued to work.

"It was the best price we could get with the way prices have been lately. I'm not happy with it, and it's not sustainable long term, but we'll be able to pay some bills."

The books were open for any of the siblings to see. They all had a share in the farm, which Ezra hadn't been entirely sure was a good idea. Trying to split something twelve ways was bound to be complicated. But, so far it had worked. At some point they were probably going to have to do something else. But for now, he was happy that the family could stay together, and they could all work and play and be around each other. It hadn't exactly been a dream of his, but his parents had wanted that for them. Part of the problem with the ranch in Wyoming was it was too small.

He wasn't sure North Dakota was any better. It was a lot bigger, but it seemed like it would be a lot harder to make money here. Hopefully the dude ranch would take off, but that wasn't his area. People and talking weren't his strengths.

But Alaska had given him grace.

Actually, he found he didn't mind talking to her. She seemed to care about him. Or maybe she just seemed interested. Or maybe she was just good at working him. He didn't like that last thought, but the fact remained that she did have a lot of experience. Experience he didn't have. And that was where she was going to need to give him grace.

He could ask someone, and like he told her, he could Google it, but neither of those two things sounded good to him. It wasn't something he wanted to talk to his siblings about; it wasn't exactly something a man ever talked about. Not in the context that he wanted to talk about it.

Maybe it was just best that, like Alaska said, they learned about each other together.

Beyond that, he probably ought to let her in on the working of the farm. He didn't want to push her into a job right away, but maybe she'd be happier if she felt like she had a place. She'd done such a good job of organizing the wedding…

"Do you think our sisters will have a problem with Alaska joining them? They'd give her a job?"

"Yeah." Caleb's word was easy, casual. "Are you sure Alaska wants a job? She's got two children, and that's a lot of work for one person. Maybe she doesn't want anything extra."

"I just thought having her do something would make her feel more included on the place."

"It might. Why don't you talk to her about it. I can't tell you what Alaska wants."

"No. I was asking you about our sisters. I'll find out what Alaska wants."

He was a little irritated. And he knew it came out in his voice. He didn't want his brother to think that he was asking for advice about his wife. He definitely didn't want his wife to hear that he was asking for advice about her from his brother. What did his brother know anyway? Not that he didn't respect his brother and think that he knew a lot about some things. Just... Caleb had never been married, so he could hardly give Ezra advice.

They worked steadily, with Ezra taking a moment or two once in a while to look up at the bright blue sky, see the puffy clouds go by, and watch the grasses bend in the wind. Part of what he loved about farming was being able to be outside and enjoy the wide open spaces. It seemed silly to do it, and yet not enjoy it.

The funny thing was, he wanted Alaska to be enjoying it with him.

As they finished up, rolling up what was left of the wire and putting their tools away, he said to Caleb, "Think I'm going to take tomorrow off."

"What?" Caleb said, probably more from shock than because he hadn't actually heard.

"I'm going to take tomorrow off." Ezra stated it like it shouldn't be a surprise to anyone.

"But I can't remember the last time you took a day off."

"I know. That means it's time."

"All right. I was okay with this whole marriage thing, but if she's going to turn you into someone I don't recognize, I might develop a stronger opinion about it."

"No. I just think that... Dad always made time for mom. You know?"

"Their marriage was a good example. Maybe that's why I'm not married. I can't find anyone who's like mom. She seemed to be the perfect mix of humor and fun and responsibility and work ethic. And she knew how to make Dad smile."

"She knew how to make our lives fun as well. I know she disciplined us, but she must have done it when we were little, because I don't remember it."

"Mom always said that if you could train a child when they were little, you wouldn't have a problem with them when they were older."

"I remember her disciplining the younger ones, so, I guess it's true. As they got older, they needed it less and less."

"Yeah. She was quite a lady. I wish..." Ezra knew that there was no point in wishing. Wishes didn't make anything better, and they didn't make anything happen either. His dad always said that if you wanted something, you'd better be prepared to work for it.

He supposed that applied to a marriage as well. If he wanted a good marriage, he'd better be prepared to work for it.

He thought he was. But, part of having a good marriage was spending time together. At least... That's what he thought. Was that right?

He supposed they were just going to have to figure it out. The thought made him smile. Because, the more time he spent with Alaska, the more time he wanted to spend with her. And he didn't mind figuring things out with her. She brought a perspective into his life that he hadn't realized he needed and hadn't known he was missing in the first place.

"Hey, have you heard from Asher?" Caleb asked as they got into the ATV and started driving back toward the farm.

"No." He hadn't even given Asher thought, which scared him a little. He was the head of the family, and he should have an idea of what was going on. Asher was a grown man, of course, and could take care of himself. But everyone should have someone who cared about them and wanted to know that things are going well with them. For now, that was Ezra's job.

"I think I'll call him." Caleb said.

Ezra waited while Caleb dialed his number. But apparently Asher didn't answer, and Caleb left a message.

"I don't think he has service at the cabin." Typically when Asher went, he'd drive down the mountain a bit and return any calls at the end of the day.

Ezra was not worried. Asher was more than capable of taking care of himself. And Sondra. As difficult as Sondra could be. But, he did feel a little responsibility.

"I hope she didn't eat him," Caleb said as he hung up the phone.

"You better watch it. She might end up being your sister-in-law."

"You just got married to someone else yesterday. Don't tell me you're one of those."

"Asher, you crackerhead," Ezra said, like it was obvious. Which to him, it was. He'd seen the way Asher looked at Sondra.

"No. Asher and Sondra? No way."

Ezra just lifted his brows and continued to drive. It seemed very realistic to him. Why else would Asher have volunteered to take Sondra out of the way? Not because Asher wanted Alaska to be part of the family.

And there it was again, all of his thoughts came back to Alaska. Maybe, when he got a chance, he would reconfigure the work schedule he had in his head and allow himself to be doing something that would keep him closer to the house. It wasn't necessarily his concern for Alaska's safety, although that definitely played a part in his brain, but he just wanted to be near her. The thought scared him a little, but it also made him smile.

Chapter Twenty-One

"I can't wait to have children," Ellen said with a smile as she sat on the floor of Alaska's little house and played with Eugene.

"You're a natural with them. Eugene loves you. And he doesn't always warm up to people very quickly," Alaska said. Ellen looked up, smiling at her friend as her baby drank a bottle.

"Ezra is used to a lot of kids. He probably wants to have ten or twelve just like his parents. I think that would be so awesome," Ellen said. Ellen couldn't help but dream. The idea of growing up in a large family was one she had held close to her heart. She had ended up being an only child, after her mother had died, and her uncle had brought her to America to raise on his own.

Of course, her uncle had gotten married, and they had two children, but Ellen was so much older than her half siblings, that she felt more like an aunt or a nanny to them than their sister. But, she always hoped that when she got married, they could have a lot of kids. Twelve would not be too many.

"So you guys are going to have children right away?" Alaska asked, and it was a casual question.

Ellen nodded eagerly. "I hope so. I mean, we have to take what God gives us, but I'm really hoping we can start right away, and Travis is down for that too." They were more blessed than someone else might be, because Travis had spent the last eight years working hard and he'd managed to be extremely successful. He wouldn't have to work another day in his life if he didn't want to, and they would have plenty of money to raise as many children as Ellen wanted to have.

"You know, Ezra's mom had a helper. Nelda. Do you know her?"

"I've seen her at church. I wasn't quite sure what the relationship was to the family. I asked her once, and she answered me, but I didn't know her well enough to understand everything she was saying, if that makes sense."

"It does. I don't think that it's easy to qualify her relationship, because she treats the kids' children as her grandchildren. They call her a nanny, but I think she was more. Almost like a member of the family."

"That would make things a lot easier. To have someone who was so dedicated to you and your children that they become part of the family."

"Exactly. And it would make it easier whenever someone has to watch your children. Nelda has kept mine a couple of times, and she was like you and Travis. I felt like her main concern was for the kids. That... Isn't something you get every time someone watches your kids."

Ellen figured Alaska would know. After all, Alaska had given Eugene to someone at the same time she had given Alice to Travis, and whoever had kept Eugene had not done a good job. She didn't think that Eugene had been abused or anything, but the person who was supposed to be watching him, had quit midway through.

Ellen knew raising children was a big job, and while it made her a little nervous, she knew that people had been raising children for centuries, and if they could do it, she could do it too. Her biggest concern was raising them to love the Lord. That didn't seem to be a given in today's world, and it's what she wanted for her kids with all of her heart.

"I bet you wish Ezra's mom was here so you could talk to her."

Alaska seemed like she hadn't even considered that idea, and Ellen remembered that Alaska hadn't been married for very long.

Of course, neither had she.

"That would be really nice. I know I have some questions I

wouldn't mind asking someone who has experience. You know, things you can't really talk about with just anyone."

"Yeah," Ellen said, thinking about how she'd found out this morning that there wasn't going to be a wedding night conception. Not for her.

But, she wasn't discouraged. She and Travis hadn't been married that long, and they had plenty of time to practice, as Travis called it. He hadn't seemed disappointed that they would need to keep practicing. In fact, he seemed a little happy about it. Ellen didn't think it was because they weren't having a baby right away, but it was because exactly what he said, he liked practicing.

Ellen didn't mind that either. In fact, it was something she looked forward to, not just because she enjoyed it, but because she felt it gave the relationship she had with Travis more depth and meaning. And definitely closeness. That was probably why it was called intimacy.

"You do it!" Eugene said, handing her the truck that he had been running back and forth on the floor.

"I get to drive the truck?" she asked, and he smiled real big and nodded his head up and down. He was adorable, and Ellen couldn't wait until it was her turn to be a mom.

"You know, anytime you need someone to watch the children, I'd be happy to," Ellen said, and not just because she loved children. But, that was the main reason she had come over. To bring a casserole, and to offer to help Alaska with the kids if she needed it. They were both newly married, but as Alaska's situation was a little different than Ellen's, and Ellen thought that maybe she would need a little bit of time to develop a relationship with her husband. If Ellen could help by watching the kids, she would.

"Well you know that I trust you with them," Alaska said. "I really can't thank you and Travis enough for what you did for Alice. I... Can't believe how much my life has changed in such a short time."

"That happens with the Lord. Things look impossible, and then all the sudden, they happen. And you can totally see how everything makes sense, but you remember how hopeless they felt before God opened the door."

"That's a perfect description of how I feel. But maybe, I just feel like

I need to grow a little more. I don't feel worthy of Ezra, if that makes sense."

"It does make sense, but I don't think you need to worry about it. First of all, Ezra isn't a judgy person. And secondly, he wouldn't have married you if he didn't want to. I've wondered about that a little. He's so serious and methodical. It seems crazy that he did something that seems like such a spur of the moment thing. I think you'll find he really likes you."

Alaska smiled a little secret smile, and Ellen figured she probably already was finding out that Ezra did truly like her.

Ellen continued to play with Eugene for a little bit while she and Alaska talked, but she had chores to get home to, and she didn't want to keep Alaska from her work.

She left with a smile on her face, and excitement in her heart. Her turn to be a mother would be soon, she was sure.

Chapter Twenty-Two

Alaska watched Ellen leave. It was new, this feeling of having friends. Having people who cared about her, and would help her if she needed it, not because she was going to pay them, or because they were going to get something from it, but because they liked her, and wanted to do something kind to her. That was...one of the best feelings in the world.

Although, she would take the feeling she had while kissing Ezra over that any day.

She'd been bitterly disappointed when he continued his insistence on sleeping on the couch.

Part of her wanted to see if she could talk him into doing what she wanted, or maybe not talk. *Kiss* him into doing what she wanted. But, that didn't seem like a good way to start a marriage, trying to get her way by using her feminine wiles.

So, she pushed back on the idea that she could probably get him to do what she wanted using the weapons at her disposal. But again, she didn't want to think about them as weapons, so she shoved it aside, and decided that she would wait and assume that Ezra knew what he was doing.

Glancing at the clock, and seeing it was two hours until lunch, she grabbed the diaper and took Alice to the spot where Eugene played with his trucks so she could change her diaper beside him.

She'd just gotten Alice's pants put back on when there was a sound that made her glance up.

The door burst open at that moment, and Chalmer burst in.

Her eyes grew wide. Rex she might have expected, although she thought that as long as he wasn't on drugs, he wouldn't venture out to the ranch. And even if he were, now that everyone knew to watch for him, she didn't think that he would make it the whole way to her without someone knowing.

But Chalmer. This she hadn't thought of.

"Oh my goodness, if it isn't the mother of my children." Chalmer said, in a voice that wasn't friendly. Not even a little.

"Chalmer. I didn't expect you." She couldn't think of anything else to say. Although that felt like the understatement of the year. He hadn't been the slightest bit interested in his children, not in paying for them, not doing anything with them at all.

"Of course you didn't. But, surely you know, that now that you're married to someone who is one of the wealthiest people in the state of North Dakota, that I would be here for my share."

"No. I hadn't thought that. And, I don't think that Ezra is as wealthy as you seem to think he is."

"How could he not be? Look at this spread. This isn't something that happens without a massive amount of money."

"Well I suppose if you ask him, you could find out for yourself."

"I'm not asking."

"You're not?" Alaska said, as she carefully got herself off the floor, and picked Eugene up, who had been clinging to her since Chalmer walked in the door. For some reason, Eugene had always been petrified of Chalmer, even when he was a baby.

"No. You are."

"No. I couldn't ask him for money. I know that —" she broke off abruptly. The little bit she knew about the finances on the ranch was information that she thought she should not share with Chalmer, even if she thought that it might keep him from being misguided in the amount of money he thought the ranch had.

"Oh, yes, you can. You can, and you will." He smiled evilly. "If you don't, I'm not going to bring your baby back to you."

"No. You don't get to take my children."

"I think we should share custody. And it's time for my turn. Are you going to deny a father the right to see his child?"

"Yes. I am. You lied to me. You told me you weren't married. I never would have been with you to begin with if I had known that you had a wife and a child at home."

"Whatever. You can pretend that you have values and morals all day long if you want to, but we both know that you don't."

"I do. When it comes to that. I mean, I've changed."

He laughed, like the idea of her changing, of her being better than what she used to be was ludicrous.

She couldn't believe she'd ever been with this person. The difference between him and Ezra was so stark. Ezra had given her all the grace she needed to cover all the mistakes that she'd made, and he believed that she truly was trying to be better. Not only believed, but encouraged her in that direction.

Now she actually was scared. What if he did take her children? Did he have a right to them?

She knew the ranch didn't have an overabundance of money. So if he didn't think he could take the children, and he wanted money for them... What if Ezra couldn't pay?

"You're not on their birth certificates. I never put you there. So I think that means that you don't have any right at all to them."

"I can demand a paternity test."

"I guess you'd have to go to court for that." She figured that would take money. Surely. And maybe he wouldn't want to put the expense out in order to claim the kids. And then she thought of something. "And, if you prove that you're the father, then you should be paying for your children. There's a whole bunch of years you didn't pay a cent for. You owe me."

"Now you just wait here a minute. I shouldn't have to pay for these kids. It wasn't my idea for you to get pregnant."

"You were there too," she said, with a little bit of irony in her voice, although she was too scared to really appreciate it to the fullness that it deserved. Eugene squirmed, and she realized her hand had tightened around him, until she was pressing both of her children against her body. Like that would somehow keep them safe.

"I don't think that's legal." He lifted his chin and crossed his arms over his chest.

He'd come in, but he hadn't made any effort to interact with his children, or to touch them in any way. That made Alaska a little bit sad, but not too terribly much. Ezra was more than willing to be a father to her kids, and she appreciated that more than she could say. Probably more than anything else he had done.

"Is it legal for you to take your child and then demand payment from my husband in order to get him back?" she said, saying a small prayer that God would give her the courage to continue to face him. She felt like maybe her words were getting through, and Chalmer was rethinking the whole idea of kidnapping his kids.

"I never said it was. You're the one that's all the sudden doing everything according to the law."

She pressed her lips together and didn't say anything

"Now. Are you going to hand them over, or am I going to have to take them from you by force?"

"I don't want you to take them at all," she said, racking her brain for what she could do to try to thwart him, but short of putting a child down and picking up a weapon, she was stuck. And she wouldn't be able to outrun him with a child on each hip.

"You didn't answer my question. Give me the kid."

"No. They're mine. And you're not taking them."

She'd no sooner said that, then Chalmer took several quick steps forward and shoved her as hard as he could. She hadn't been expecting it, and then she was concerned about making sure Alice didn't land under her when she fell, so she tried to land on her back, so that she didn't hurt either one of her children, but in the process, she twisted to the side and struck her head on the corner of the table. The blow stunned her to the point where she couldn't make her arm hold tight, and he was able to grab Alice.

"You can keep that one. He'll be a pain in the butt, sniffling the whole time."

Chalmer walked toward the door. "Get your husband to pay, and I'll bring her back."

Alaska tried to shake off the fog and the blackness pulled at her vision. Eugene had fallen out of her arm, and lay crying on the floor. She struggled to her hands and knees, with the sole intent of going after Chalmer to get Alice back.

She wasn't fast enough, couldn't make herself move, couldn't see through the pain and fuzziness in her head.

"You know my number. Text me when you have the money." Chalmer laughed, then walked toward the door. "And, if I see the police, I'm going to tell them you wouldn't let me see my children, so I had to come get one myself."

With a last laugh, he put a hand on the doorknob and walked out.

Chapter Twenty-Three

"You need to come back to the house right away. Someone took the baby."

Ezra adjusted the phone to his ear, because surely, he hadn't heard right. "What?" He asked Phoebe, even though he was already starting to stride toward the ATV. He didn't even bother to pick up any of his things.

"Is Alaska okay?" he asked before Phoebe could answer his first question.

"He shoved her, and she fell and hit her head. I think that's the only way he got the baby, but other than a huge headache, and being petrified, she's fine."

"I'm on my way."

He started the ATV, and had driven about ten feet before he heard Caleb shout. "Hey! Hold up!"

Ezra slowed but didn't stop as Caleb jumped in the other side, slamming the door shut.

"Did you call the police?" he asked.

"Yes. They said they would watch for him on the road, maybe try to intercept him on his way back to Sweet Water. They had an officer on duty near there."

"All right."

His hands shook and it seemed like the ATV was crawling while time flew by. He also felt like a failure. Alaska had married him for the purpose of keeping herself and her children safe. And this was the second time that someone had gotten onto the ranch.

"He was driving the same color car as Ellen was, and we assume that when Ellen drove away from the ranch, he drove in the gates before they closed. Ellen wouldn't have known to try to keep anyone out."

"Yeah. All right." Well that answered that question. But still, he felt guilty and responsible.

He punched off, and threw his phone down on the seat beside him. What more could he do? How many people were going to be after his wife? And their children? Although Chalmer was technically the likely father. It sounded like Ezra was going to need to get a lawyer and get on it. Figure out what rights Chalmer might have, and possibly see if he would give up those rights. Ezra was fairly certain he didn't care about the kids, he just wanted money. Unfortunately, that was something that Ezra didn't have a lot of at the moment.

They would be getting the money for the calves they just sold, but there were bills that needed to be paid, and he could hardly take money from the ranch to pay for his personal problems. Although, he was pretty sure that his siblings would rally around him, and would want to make sure his wife was safe.

Still, he'd feel selfish taking money they didn't have to buy off someone whose problems he brought on himself when he insisted on marrying Alaska.

Lord, I don't know what to do.

There were lots of times where he had prayed a prayer like that to God. So many times in his life where he didn't know what to do, but this felt so much more... Dangerous.

Scary even. But that was mostly because short of tying Alaska to him, and carrying their kids around everywhere they went, he couldn't have her with him twenty-five, seven, and he felt like she should be safe in his home on his ranch. The fact that she wasn't, made him feel like he needed to adjust everything he had been thinking.

Caleb didn't say anything else, and Ezra didn't really pay attention to him anyway. He careened into the yard, jerked to a stop in front of his house, and grabbed his phone before jumping out of the side-by-side, running in the house, needing to see for himself that Alaska was okay.

Phoebe had said she was. He knew there was nothing he could do by rushing to her side, but he felt like he needed to. She was probably beside herself because Alice was missing, and Ezra couldn't even think about that. Did the man take a car seat? Was their baby safe? Had he thrown her somewhere? Someone like that... He didn't think that Chalmer had much of a criminal record, and he wasn't sure whether drugs were involved, but he didn't really think that he'd throw his own child out of the car window, but, all sorts of crazy ideas were going through Ezra's head at the moment, and that seemed just as likely as anything else.

"Alaska," he said, slowing as he came up on her, sitting at the kitchen table with an ice pack held to her head, Priscilla on one side of her with her arm slung protectively over her shoulder, and Phoebe on the other, while Ada played with Eugene at the sink trying to keep him occupied so that he wasn't asking for his mother.

Alaska probably would have been happier holding him in her lap, but Ezra didn't say that, he simply walked across the kitchen floor, and knelt on one knee beside her, taking both her hands in his and looking up into her face. He winced as she lifted the ice pack off, and he saw a big knot on the side of her temple.

"Sorry," he said, knowing that everything that had happened was his fault. He should have stayed home. Should have taken the danger more seriously. Realized that it wasn't just going to be Rex. But that Chalmer would want to try to extort money from Alaska as well. It made him mad the men who had used her.

"It's not your fault," she said, and her voice sounded wobbly, but there was no doubt of the relief that was on her face and he assumed that it was because he was there.

She put one hand on either side of his face and smiled.

"I feel so much better now that you're here."

"I never should have left."

"You have to run the farm. You have work to do. I get it."

"None of that is more important than you, your safety, and the safety of our children." He brought her hands to his lips, and pressed them close. Relief that she was okay, fear for Alice warred in his body, and he felt the need to get up to walk around, to do something. He hated just sitting around. But, if they were going to go through the police, that was what was going to happen. He had to let someone else do their job, while he prayed. That was all he could do. Other than staying beside Alaska and making sure that no one else was able to touch her.

"Pheebs and I talked about it, and we thought that maybe you two would want to have a day or two together. But, we were hoping that Alaska would start working with us. I know Claudia said that she had asked about cooking, and if that's her interest, there's plenty of cooking to do. I mean, she would be with us all the time. That would help keep her safe."

"That'd be great. But yeah, I guess I probably want to spend the rest of the day with her. Tomorrow too. We'll see how this turns out. I need to spend some time on the phone with my lawyer. I already was in contact with him for the PFA and I suppose he can handle this."

"Chalmer doesn't want custody. He just wants money."

"Right. It can't look good, being that he is using his supposed rights as a parent to manipulate that."

"Does he have any rights?" Priscilla asked.

"I'm not sure what the law says about that. We'll have to look into it."

"I think he's so desperate for money that if we offered him something, he'd give up his rights, legally, and then we wouldn't have to worry about this again." There. He put it out there. So they could be thinking about it.

"I know the ranch doesn't have much," Tobias spoke, and Ezra looked up in surprise. He hadn't even realized that Tobias had come in. Tobias, more than any of his siblings, usually spent a lot of time alone. He was happy to work alone, didn't always come to the table for meals, and was happy in the cabin he'd lived in all winter on the far side of the ranch.

"I think that whatever we have, we should make sure that this gets taken care of. We can't have someone coming on the property, taking

Alaska's children." Ada spoke up, from where she stood at the sink, running water and letting Eugene play in the stream that came out. A clever way to distract the little boy, because he was no longer fussing for his mom.

He also appreciated Ada's support.

"I knew when I married her that everyone would rally around her and help me protect her. I...wasn't expecting it to cost us money."

"I feel terrible. Please don't make the ranch suffer because of me. But, I really would like to figure out how to get Alice back." Alaska wasn't crying, but she clung to his hands, holding them tightly so tightly her knuckles were white.

"We'll get her. If it's possible, we'll do it." He didn't go into all the things that had gone through his mind, all of the crazy situations that could happen, all the ways that a baby could be hurt and even...killed.

"Ezra. Were you not listening to me?" Tobias spoke again, slight irritation in his voice. "I know the ranch doesn't have much, but I do. I've been saving for a long time, and I don't know how much the man wants, but I have close to fifty thousand in my account, and we can offer all of it to him in exchange for him signing away his parental rights."

Ezra couldn't believe it. Where had Tobias gotten that kind of money? And then, as he thought about it, he realized that Tobias really had never spent any money. Anything he ever earned, he probably saved. He never went anywhere, he never did anything, and he hadn't even bought a truck, which was the first thing that Ezra had done when he had had enough money saved up.

But Tobias had always been content to keep to himself, quiet, unassuming, and, after the things that he had gone through, Ezra couldn't blame him.

"I couldn't take your money," Ezra said. Knowing as he said it, that for Alaska, he probably would.

"I'm not giving it to you. I'm giving it to Alaska."

He looked down as Alaska's eyes widened, and Ezra squeezed her hands. This was his family. And, while he was still petrified for Alice, he was proud that his siblings had always rallied around each other. Now he was the one who needed them, and they hadn't hesitated to step forward.

"Thank you," she said, emotion in every syllable.

"It might not take that much. It might take a lot less. I wouldn't let anyone know how much you have. Maybe we can get away with paying him a lot less. I would feel bad about saying we're trying to get a bargain for someone's parental rights, except it's obvious that they don't mean anything to him."

Ezra felt a little bit bad for the man. He didn't know what he was missing out on. Alaska had a beautiful heart, and she was honest and loyal. And, from what Ezra could see, she wanted to do everything in her power to make sure their marriage was a success.

Chalmer should have taken her while he could get her. Of course, he had never been free to pursue Alaska, since he had been married and lying to her the entire time.

They talked a little more, coming up with a plan, which included Ezra calling the lawyer as soon as he pulled himself away from Alaska, and figuring out what they could do and what rights Chalmer had.

There was also the possibility that if Chalmer really didn't have any parental rights, the police would charge him with kidnapping, and child endangerment, and hopefully a whole slew of other things that Ezra, who was a rancher, and not involved in law enforcement at all, could never come up with on his own.

He would want them to throw the book at Chalmer, just to keep Alaska safe. Not necessarily because he wanted to punish the man.

Although, if one hair on Alice's head was harmed, it would be hard for Ezra to remember that he was a Christian and was supposed to forgive. Because he would want revenge.

He hoped it didn't come to that, because he knew what was right. God said vengeance was His. But, sometimes it seemed God moved too slowly, and Ezra wouldn't want to wait. He would want Chalmer to be punished immediately.

Regardless, he stood, promising Alaska he would be back, before he went outside, stood on the porch and called his lawyer.

Chapter Twenty-Four

"It's the police," Phoebe said as her phone began to ring.

Alaska's head throbbed, and her brain still felt fuzzy, but she straightened up in her chair immediately, wincing against the sharp pain that shot down her temple and felt like it came bursting out her elbow.

"Answer it!" she said as Phoebe swiped.

Please let Alice be okay. Please.

She couldn't get any more words out than that, but God knew what she was asking, begging, for.

"Hello?" Phoebe said as she put the phone to her ear and spoke in such a calm voice that Alaska wanted to grab her.

"Oh, thank God," she said. Then she shifted the phone down just slightly and spoke over the receiver to Alaska. "They have Chalmer in custody, and they have Alice. She's fine. They want to know how much she usually eats and they're making her a bottle."

"Four ounces," Alaska said, relief making her weak so it was hard to sit up. She wanted to set her head on the table and cry, now that it was over. She hadn't wanted to cry before. Maybe she'd been too scared.

"They don't want to bring her back, because she doesn't have a car seat. We can go get her anytime."

"All right. I'll be right there."

"No." Caleb put a hand on her arm. "Ezra will die if you go anywhere without him. Just hold on until he's off the phone."

"Wait." Phoebe spoke, and then she held the phone back up to her mouth. "That would be awesome. Thank you so much." There was a pause and then she said, "All right. We'll see you in a bit."

She swiped off.

"They're bringing her out. They found a car seat in the back room."

"Right now?" Alaska said, wanting to see her baby that second, make sure that she was okay.

"Yeah. They'll talk to us when they get here. But they have Chalmer in custody, so I assume they weren't buying his idea that because he was the dad, he could just take her whenever he wanted to."

"I hope not. I feel like even though their mine, it's like...like I'm not worthy to be their mom and anyone can see that and they'll just take them from me," she said. She couldn't help it, she covered her face with her hands and started crying.

"You've been very strong, but this is excruciating," Phoebe said as she put her arms around her on one side and Priscilla hugged her on the other, and Alaska cried, but felt comforted at the same time, because there were people who were standing with her. It made a huge difference in a person's life when they had people who they knew they could depend on. She'd never had that before. That was something Ezra had given her that she would always be grateful for.

She didn't cry for very long, and thankfully, the pain meds that they'd given her kicked in, and her head quit sending sharp pain that seemed to knife throughout her body.

She took Eugene from Ada, and he was content to sit on her lap holding a truck while she held him as tight as she could.

It was at least fifteen minutes before Ezra walked back in.

His face looked as serious as it always did, but it didn't look angry, or frustrated, and Alaska allowed hope to blossom in her chest. Maybe things weren't going to turn out as terribly as what she thought they would.

For some reason, she always went to the worst case scenario, thinking gloom and doom on everything.

"Hey. You don't look quite as bad as you did earlier," Ezra said, like it had been an hour or two since he'd seen her last, instead of fifteen minutes.

"They have Alice. The police are bringing her out. Chalmer is in custody, and they're going to talk to us when they get here." All the words tumbled out, all the things that she wanted to share with him, because there wasn't anyone else she wanted to talk to.

She knew Ezra wanted the best for her, and for her children as well, and somehow telling him was the most important thing.

Sure enough, a big smile broke over his face, and he came over and knelt down in front of her again, taking her hands like he had before.

"That's great news," he said.

She nodded, and she leaned forward. "Thank you."

"I didn't do anything. In fact, it's all my fault that Chalmer was even able to get —"

She put a finger over his lips. "For your family. For you. I... I would be dealing with this on my own if it weren't for you. I don't know what you saw in me, I don't know why, but thank you. For taking me. Marrying me. Giving me your family."

His eyes glowed, as he understood what she was saying, and knew that his family had accepted her, and she appreciated it.

"Alright. I guess you're welcome, although I can't really take credit for them. That would be my parents."

"You are the big brother," she whispered.

"Well, it looks like everything is in good shape here. I would like to know what the police say, but I have some work to do, and think Ezra has things well in hand. I'm heading out," Phoebe said, with Priscilla beside her. Ada left with the girls as well, and Caleb came over and put a hand on Ezra's shoulder.

"I'll keep an eye on things. I'm sorry I wasn't more diligent, or I should have made sure that we all were more diligent."

"It's my fault. But we're not going to blame anyone, we're just going to try to do better." Ezra nodded his head, and Caleb jerked his chin before he left.

Tobias came over, standing silently in the room. He was a bit of a mystery to Alaska, but she couldn't be anything but grateful to him because he'd offered them so much money, just to get her child back.

The child that he had no attachment to, other than his brother wanted to adopt her.

"What did the lawyer say?"

Alaska listened as Ezra explained the different tactics the lawyer said would work. While he didn't feel that Chalmer had any parental rights, he could sue for them, demand a paternity test, and make their lives generally miserable.

The lawyer had suggested that if they could use some kind of buyout to entice Chalmer to give up his parental rights, that would be the easiest, and potentially least expensive way. It would also be foolproof, because once Chalmer signed his rights away, he could not get them back. And he could not have any say or presence in Alice or Eugene's life unless Alaska said it was okay. He also said that he would start proceedings for Ezra to be able to adopt both children.

There were a few additional details, but Alaska didn't care. Everything was going to work out. She could hardly believe it.

"All right. You just let me know what you need. The money is sitting in my account, and I can't think of a better way to spend it."

"You probably were interested in building a house."

"What for? There's just me." He didn't say anything else, but turned and walked out.

"It seems like he's hurting," Alaska said as the door closed behind him.

"Yeah. He... He's had some hard times. With some people that he trusted I guess. It was painful, and I don't think he ever really recovered."

Alaska was curious for the details, but Ezra didn't seem inclined to give them to her at the moment, and she really didn't care. She just wanted her family together.

It felt like forever until the police pulled in. Ezra went to the door to open it and let them in, while Alaska moved from the couch in the living room to the kitchen. Eugene would have been happy playing in the room, but she convinced him to bring his toys out, so he could play at her feet and not be separated from her.

When Ezra came in, carrying Alice in her car seat, Alaska jumped up and ran over, looking at her baby who slept so soundly, so peacefully, like the entire morning hadn't been an emotional roller coaster for her mother.

"My goodness. I knew she was okay, but it makes my heart so happy to just lay eyes on her."

The officer looked familiar to her, and she'd probably seen him before, perhaps under circumstances where she was not quite on the right side of the law. Not that she had a criminal record, but up until this point in her life, the police were not the good guys. They were the ones who tried to keep her from doing what she wanted to do.

"Thank you so much, Officer. And thank you for bringing her to me. I'm so grateful."

"Not a problem. We were on the verge of drawing straws to see who was going to have to change her diaper. Then we just decided that if we could find a car seat, we'd bring her out. That seemed easier than doing the diaper thing." He seemed like a friendly person, with a fresh ruddy face and bright blue eyes. His back was straight and he obviously took his job very seriously.

"We have Chalmer in custody, and we're going to try to throw the book at him if we can. Keep him as long as we can, and hopefully that will give you guys time to put some kind of plan in place in case he tries it again. I obviously can't keep him any longer than what the law allows."

"We understand. I... I might be in to talk to him. We do have a plan, and basically what he wants is money, so we'll give him that if he gives up any right to the children."

"That'll solve it. Although, I feel like you probably have the law on your side. It'll just take a little while to churn through all the red tape."

"That's what my lawyer said. I think we're going to take the fast route, although we haven't really discussed it." Ezra looked at Alaska with his brows raised, and she nodded.

The policeman stayed for just a bit more, giving a few details of the arrest, before he left.

For the first time that day, Alaska was alone with Ezra and her children. Probably being alone should make her scared, but as long as Ezra was there, she knew he would do whatever was necessary in order to protect her. And she appreciated that. It made her feel safe. Even if there wasn't a big crowd of people around.

They made lunch, although Alaska wasn't hungry. Ezra ate, and so did Eugene. And then they put both kids to bed, and went back down to the living room.

"I've been trying to figure out a way that we can work things so that you never leave me. I... I can't just stay in the house all day, and I know you can't haul the kids around all the time. Maybe once we get this Chalmer thing figured out, we won't have any more issues, but... For me anyway, I'd like to have you pretty close."

"I'm not going to turn down extra time with you. I have to admit to being petrified today, but I also knew, in my heart, that whatever happened, God was in control. I think that while it's smart to take safety precautions, we can't just upend our lives. We have to admit that all the things we do will never be enough if God isn't on our side, protecting us."

"Wow. That was really good. I knew that. But... I guess I put a lot of responsibility on my shoulders to take care of you."

"And I appreciate it. I feel safe when you're around. But I also know that you're human. You can't be everywhere all at once, and you can't run this ranch if you have to babysit me all the time."

"I don't consider it babysitting. I consider it an honor and a privilege to get to have you."

"Really?" she said, and she knew she shouldn't have the flirty smile that wanted to break out on her lips, but she did.

"Really." He returned her smile.

They grinned at each other for a few minutes, before he seemed to shake himself.

"Anyway, I'm going to try to work close to the house for the next few days, but I already told Caleb I was taking tomorrow off. I was hoping that you and the kids might enjoy going for a picnic. I know they're kind of young, and honestly, I'd rather have just you. I feel like... Like I want to spend a little time with just you and me. But, I don't think I will let the children out of my sight, even with Nelda, who would do a great job, and who I know would defend them with her life."

"Don't you think it's a God thing again?" Alaska asked, almost unable to believe that she would be willing to allow the children out of her sight. After the huge scare they had today, she thought she would never feel comfortable with them not being immediately beside her.

"Yeah. I think you're right."

"I don't really want to leave them, but I also think that it's important that you and I spend time together. I agree with you there."

He nodded. "Maybe I can see if Caleb will stick around the house tomorrow and keep an eye on Nelda as she watches the kids. How will that be?"

"That sounds great."

"You know, we decided that we would talk to some ladies in town because you didn't think that you could be a good wife. I guess I feel like you don't really need to do that. You've already been better to me than I deserve, and I don't think the ladies in town could teach you much of anything."

"Oh, I think they could. And I'm always willing to learn. I always want to be better. But, it means so much to me to hear you say that you think I'm going to be okay. I want to be a good wife."

"And I want to be a good husband."

"I think part of being a good husband is not sleeping on the couch," she said, with her brows raised.

He grinned a little, and she reminded herself that she was not going to do anything to try to change his mind. Although, she supposed it didn't hurt to remind him every once in a while of what she wanted, just in case he might decide that he wanted the same thing.

Her heart just about leapt out of her throat when he said, "I think you're right."

A smile spread across her face, and happiness seemed to burst inside of her as she stepped forward and wrapped her arms around him. She lifted her face, and his head was already lowering.

That kiss was every bit as good as the kiss the night before. And she really didn't want it to end, but he pulled back and he said, "You know, I never believed in love at first sight. And I think I would probably be the last person in the world that anyone would think would ever fall in love that fast. But, there was something about you from the first time I saw you. Something different. Something that pulled me. I don't think it was a wrong feeling. In fact, I think it just might have been the Lord saying that you are perfect for me. I love you."

She caught her breath. She hadn't expected him to say anything like that. It definitely took her by surprise. But, it was a good surprise. The very best kind.

"I love you too. Because, I think it would be impossible not to. Not just because you've given me more than I ever thought anyone could, but because I admire you, and I can't think of anyone that I've ever enjoyed spending time with more. Or talking to. I know you've done a lot for me, I don't know if I can ever make it up to you, but I'm going to try."

"You don't need to try to do anything. Or make anything up. You are perfect just the way you are."

He lowered his head, and kissed her again.

Chapter Twenty-Five

"I'm so glad Nelda loves the children. Although, when Ellen was there yesterday, she offered to watch them anytime we needed her to as well. She is so excited about becoming a mother."

"She's expecting?"

"No. I don't think so," Alaska said, as she put her arms around Ezra's waist and he started the four wheeler after adjusting the picnic basket on the rack in front of him.

There was a cooler behind them as well, with water and dessert. As soon as his sisters found out that they were going to spend the day together, they had insisted they needed to make special food. Alaska wasn't going to argue, because she wanted the day to be special for Ezra. He dismissed her when she talked about all the things he had done for her, but she truly meant it. And, if she could find the opportunity to do something extra for him, she was definitely going to take it.

"She didn't say she was anyway, she just...talked about how much she wanted to have a big family like yours. I guess she was an only child growing up."

"Yeah. She actually didn't grow up with her parents. She lived with her uncle until she got married. I think she has a couple of younger siblings, but they're not close in age, and she probably really did long for a family."

"I hope they hurry up and have children so our kids have playmates."

"Maybe my siblings will take my lead and decide to get married. It's kind of unusual in a family our size for so many of us to not be married, although with all of the things that we've been going through with the ranch and selling the one in Wyoming and losing our parents and raising our younger siblings... It makes sense."

Alaska knew that Priscilla at least had been married before. There was something going on with her children, and Alaska wasn't sure what it was. It didn't seem to be something she wanted to talk about, and Alaska didn't feel like she could push.

She would listen if Priscilla ever wanted to talk about it. She hoped someday they'd know each other well enough that she'd talk about it with her.

They rode for a while, with the farmhouse fading out of sight as well as the buildings, and what seemed like miles of fence zipping by.

He turned, driving through some unfenced fields, before a copse of cottonwood came into view.

And then Alaska remembered what he had said about his favorite spot on the farm.

It was beautiful, shady, private, secluded, and yet open with a gorgeous view of the sky and the grass that stretched in all directions.

As they stopped by the creek, she had to admit that there was something calming about the water. The way it floated in a lazy, meandering way just soothed her soul, and she assumed Ezra felt it as well.

"I don't know why I can just stare at water as it rolls along, always different. It shifts and shimmers and... It's just very relaxing. It's easy to think too."

"I can see what you're saying. I... I haven't had the opportunity to spend much time beside any creeks, and I'm looking forward to it." She narrowed her eyes. "You don't seem like the kind of person who would sit beside a stream and admire it for hours on end. But I'm glad to see that you have a little bit of a hidden part of your personality that I didn't know about."

She blushed a little because that wasn't the only hidden part of his personality that she didn't know. Last night had been...quite nice.

"Are you blushing?" he asked, the picnic basket in one hand, frozen in the air as he looked at her cheeks. A little grin spread across his face. "You are."

"Maybe. I might have been thinking about those little hidden parts of your personality that surprised me last night, in a very good way."

"Not in a very, very good way?" he asked, like he even needed to. But, she supposed in her experience, this was something that people had a tendency to be insecure about.

"Yes. Without a doubt. A very, very good way."

She lifted her brows at him, and then she turned to grab the cooler and lift it off the four wheeler, setting it beside the basket.

"I'm not the slightest bit hungry," Ezra said, straightening and putting an arm around her shoulders as they turned and looked at the creek again.

"Breakfast was only an hour ago. I'm not the slightest bit hungry either."

"I can't imagine what in the world we could do to pass the time."

She narrowed her eyes and slanted them at him. Was he flirting with her?

"I've never been skinny-dipping," she said as casually as she could.

"Wow. I was thinking we would just sit beside the creek and watch it flow, but... I think I like your idea better."

They had a good time, splashing in the water, even though it was probably too chilly out for either one of them to want to swim. But it was funny, she didn't notice the chill in the air or the water when Ezra was around.

A long time later, they spread out the blanket that they brought, and lay down on it, with her curled up against his side, one leg thrown over his, with his arm around her, as he absentmindedly stroked her arm.

"We probably ought not to lay in the sun too long. We're liable to get sunburn on bits and pieces that don't typically ever see the sun."

"That's funny. I was just lying here thinking that I hope this place is as secluded as what you claim it is. This would be an awkward way to get caught by anyone, even if we are married."

He laughed a little. "I don't think being married gives us a pass for public indecency, but this is private ground, so there's that."

"You have an awful lot of brothers and sisters."

"I'm pretty sure all of my brothers and sisters know what I'm doing today. And where I am. I think they'll let us alone. Maybe twenty years ago I might have had issues with my brothers thinking it would be funny to 'surprise us.'"

"Twenty years ago I was five." She laughed a little, but Ezra stilled beside her, and she ran a hand down his rib cage as she looked up at him. "Are you okay?"

"It just surprises me sometimes that the difference in our ages is so great. It doesn't bother me. I hope it doesn't bother you."

"I wouldn't have thought that I would find my soulmate, and he would be so much older than me. You think we'd be the same age, but that's not the way it worked."

"No. It's not, is it?" he said, smiling again.

She was happy she put his mind at ease. He'd done so much for her, although it wasn't like she was saying anything that wasn't true. She meant it with all her heart. She felt like he was her soulmate. Even odder than their age differences, were the other differences between them. Even in their interests. Here he was, at the spot where he visited often, and it was her first time beside a creek. Just that one difference, but... Their surface differences didn't seem to matter because they seem to connect on a deeper level.

"Is it cheesy to think that I feel a connection to you that I've never felt with anyone else before?" she asked, feeling a little dreamy and lazy. Sleepy. Maybe a nap would be good.

He grabbed the corner of the blanket and flicked it so it was covering her.

"I wouldn't want this person I have this deeper connection with to get sunburn on their nether regions," he murmured.

"So...that means you agree with me?"

"I told you. From the first time I saw you, I felt this irresistible pull.

Maybe it's a deeper connection, and maybe it's just the Lord. I don't know. I do know that I did not feel right with Sondra, and God protected me from marrying her, while marrying you was something that God clearly showed me was the exact right thing. And God gave me exactly what I wanted, because I want to be with you."

"And I want to be with you."

And maybe that was enough. To have someone come, someone she knew had been given to her from the Lord, who loved her, and wanted to be with her. She couldn't think of anything else that could make her more content.

Epilogue

"When are you going to let me go home?" Sondra said, as Asher came in the door with an arm load of firewood.

He'd just brought her to the cabin, they'd been there all of ten minutes, and she'd been going crazy because there was no cell phone service.

"I don't think you really want to go," he said casually, knowing that he could quite potentially face kidnapping charges.

"How could you presume to know what I do and do not want?" Sondra said, with her hands on her hips.

"I guess I'm not really presuming. But, isn't there some show that you watch where they get away in the mountains for a week and they see if they can make it without electricity or running water? Wasn't that one of your favorites a while back?"

"Big Brother in the Woods!" Sondra snapped her fingers. "You're right. I loved it. And, I really don't think that Zeke should have won. It should have been Ralph, and here's why." She started going off on the show, and Asher listened for a couple of minutes before he moved, to dump the firewood on in the box by the door.

She barely noticed that he wasn't standing in front of her anymore and kept going on about her show.

He didn't really mind listening to her talk. He'd always liked the sound of her voice when she talked to Ezra.

He arranged the wood in the box, grateful that it was spring, and the only time they'd need the fire would be to cook and at night when the temperatures dipped down as they had a tendency to do in the mountains.

He'd built this cabin years ago and spent his vacation time fixing it up. It wasn't anything special, but it gave him a place to go to have some peace and quiet away from his big family. He loved them, loved every single one of them, but sometimes a man just needed a break.

He turned back to Sondra, she was still talking, and he listened. She hadn't been any good for his brother, Ezra. Ezra was too serious, and he didn't have any interest in the things that meant so much to Sondra.

Although, Asher kind of figured that Sondra used TV as a crutch, because she was alone without it, and she viewed all of the people on the screen as her friends. He also thought that maybe that was what she saw in Ezra. She saw his big family, and wanted to be a part of it because she was lonely.

Asher felt bad for, and he also had a huge crush on her. What a terrible thing to have a crush on his brother's fiancée. Except, Ezra was married to someone else, and Sondra was no longer engaged.

Unfortunately, she had never looked at him and seen anything interesting.

He might have a week, if that, to try to see if he could convince her that there was more to him than she had noticed so far.

Join Jessie's list and be the first to know about new releases and sales on her books!

Read *A Cowboy's Secret Crush*, the next story from the Sweet View Ranch series in which Asher Clyborne's longtime secret love is about to be unveiled - whether he's ready or not.

<h1 style="text-align:center">Sneak Peek of A Cowboy's Secret Crush</h1>

He had never kidnapped anyone before.

Asher Clybourn glanced across the seat at the woman sitting beside him. He wasn't sure she had stopped talking since they left Sweet Water, North Dakota, five hours ago.

Her phone had died shortly after they crossed the line from North Dakota into Montana. Ever since then, she'd been rotating between asking him how much longer until they got there, regaling him with stories of the latest movies and TV shows she watched, and despairing that she would ever get her phone plugged in and heartbroken because she was missing all the latest of her episodes.

Asher had not told her that where they were going, there would be no electricity.

He also had not told her that he had a charger in the console of his pickup.

She stopped talking for several seconds, and he glanced over to see if she was looking at him like she needed him to answer a question she just asked.

Her eyes pointed down at her hands which were clasped in her lap, so he figured he was off the hook. But his heart was troubled, just a little, because Sondra seemed so confident, so...worldly. But that little glance showed him that maybe some of it at least was a front. He'd never seen her look more insecure.

He swallowed, tightened his hold on the steering wheel, and spoke. "There's a rest stop up ahead. Do you need to stop?"

"Can we stay for an hour or so, so I can charge my phone?" Her eyes lifted hopefully, and her voice held suppressed excitement.

"No. We can't."

He wasn't being mean. Not on purpose. But if they wanted to get to his secluded mountain cabin before dark, they couldn't spend a lot of time sitting around. Although, he was going to have to stop in the last small town and grab some things at the grocery store. His cabin was stocked with some canned food, but Sondra seemed like the kind of woman who was used to having fresh produce and some of the finer things in life around her at all times.

He could provide those things for her. But she'd always been more interested in his older brother, Ezra, and had never given him a second glance.

Of course, when they were younger, that was totally understandable since she was four years older than he was, and in high school, a girl who was four years older didn't look back at a boy who was so much younger.

But now, now that they were adults, the age difference shouldn't matter. At least in his mind, it shouldn't.

But what did he know? He and his family had spent so much time trying to get their ranch profitable, and then with his parents dying in a car accident, they had even more on their plates, he hadn't really had time to learn what might or might not be important regarding age differences.

He could tell himself that was why Sondra was in the pickup with him. Because his loyalty was to his family, and his brother needed to focus on his new wife and not have his ex-fiancée in the picture. But Asher knew, deep down, that was a lie.

She was in the pickup with him now because of the crush he'd had on her for years. He had seen an opportunity for him to spend time with her, and he hadn't wanted to pass it up.

She hadn't said anything more since he'd denied her request to charge her phone, so he prompted her. "But if you need to stop to use the restroom, we can."

"How much longer until we get there?" she asked, and for the first time, he heard a little bit of...fear in her voice.

Immediately, he worked to combat whatever issues she was having.

"It'll only be another five or so hours. As long as we don't get caught up anywhere. I'll have to stop once for fuel, but I'll probably do that when we're closer." That way, he would have as full of a tank as he could when they headed to the mountains. There was no place to grab fuel for the last forty-five minutes of their trip.

He loved his cabin because it was remote. That had been the whole selling point of the property for him. He'd spent a lot of time building the cabin, and it was pretty nice now, if he did say so himself, even if it was very rustic.

What would Sondra think of it?

"Okay. Let's stop. I can probably get a drink even if I can't charge my phone. Did I mention that I'm missing all of my great shows?" she asked, and while her composure seemed to be back, he noted that her fingers played with the seam of her jeans, folding it and unfolding it as though she were nervous or upset.

Withdrawal would do that to a person.

Sondra was so hooked on her phone, her electronics, and her fictional characters that being without them was probably difficult. Asher didn't want to pretend to know what was best for her, but he figured probably any addiction that a person had had a tendency to draw them away from the Lord. After all, the only addiction that would be acceptable would be an addiction to God and His Word. Anything else was an idol.

That was kind of hard core, and he had a few idols in his own life he constantly tried to remove.

"All right. We'll stop. If you'd like me to get you something from the vending machine while you're in the restroom, I can. I think they probably have drinks and snack items."

"Do you think they'd have a fruit cup?" she asked, looking over at him hopefully.

He'd never had an affinity for blondes, or any particular hair color, because his affinity had always been for Sondra. Since she happened to be blonde, he would have said that was his favorite hair color. Her big green eyes blinked at him, and he had to be careful not to get caught by them, since he needed to keep his focus on the road. In North Dakota, with the miles upon miles of stick-straight roads, it wasn't quite as important, but since they'd hit the foothills, the road had gotten more curvy, and while not dangerous—or treacherous, the way he might term it as they got closer to the Rockies—it still took his full attention.

He didn't need to look at her to know what she looked like, though. The blonde hair, the emerald green eyes, the high cheekbones, and the full lips.

Of course, the rest of her looked pretty good too, although she wasn't skinny but more of a full-figured kind of girl. It was exactly how he liked her, and he wouldn't want her to change at all. He wasn't even sure that Ezra had ever noticed anything about her, and he wondered if he were to call his brother right now, if Ezra would even be able to say what color her hair was.

Asher had tried hard not to be jealous of his brother.

Ezra was commanding, the leader of their family, and Asher had the utmost respect for him and didn't have any issues with anything else in his brother's life, other than the fact that Ezra had Sondra, and he'd gotten her without even trying. She had been the one to chase after him, and he had simply stood there and allowed her to catch him.

It had made Asher angry the way Ezra didn't seem to care about her at all and the way she had seemed to fawn all over him.

But now that she was in his pickup, he didn't know what to say to her. He didn't want her to know that he knew so much about her, because that would be...a dead giveaway. A person didn't learn all there was to know about someone else just for the kicks and giggles.

Of course, he said to himself that he knew everything there was to know about her, but he knew that wasn't true. He knew everything she presented to the world, but he suspected there were deep pockets of things she kept hidden from the world. He wanted to know about those places too.

"If they have one, I can get it for you. What would be your second choice?"

"I don't want to eat a bunch of junk. I'm on a diet."

"What kind of diet?" he asked, knowing there was a difference in what she'd be able to eat. He had six sisters, so he wasn't completely oblivious to the ways of women.

"It's the twenty by three thousand by six and ten, no zucchini, no bread crusts, no papayas after six o'clock waterski diet."

"I see."

"Oh, you're familiar with it? Have you seen the TV show that features Apple Ciceron? She's the star who made the diet famous. Tell me you've heard of her!"

He didn't have a clue, although...had she said something about her earlier?

"You were talking about her earlier, weren't you?"

"You remember? Well! I didn't know you were listening to me. You looked so serious. Just like Jed Writ. He is tall, dark, and handsome, a bad-boy, silent, dark stubble on his chiseled jaw guy that all the girls fall in love with. That includes me." Her smile could light up his entire world, and it did now.

"Guess he's a lucky guy then," he said, although he didn't believe in luck. He believed in God, a God that created all things and controlled the universe with His words. In his opinion, if a person was a Christian, they didn't need luck, they just needed God.

"I guess you could say that. That would be from the man's perspective. Jiminy O'Reilly is always talking about the man's perspective on *Three Boots and a Delete*. Have you seen that show?"

"No. We don't have a TV."

"Oh, that's right. That's just crazy. Can you imagine growing up without a TV? Why, TV was my best friend when I was a kid."

He suspected as much. She knew all there was to know about it, because that's all she had to do. Her parents were absent at best. She already spent a lot of time out on their ranch in Wyoming where they grew up. She seemed to love his big family, and that was why he thought that she'd thrown herself at Ezra. He hoped it wasn't some kind of undying love that she felt for his brother, but more of the way she felt when she was around their family, and she wanted that for herself.

Asher wasn't usually that astute, but he spent a lot of time studying

Sondra. She'd been at their house a good bit, and while her attention had been mostly focused on Ezra, it had been good in a way for Asher since he had been able to study her without her knowing.

Of course, the more he figured out about her, the deeper his feelings ran.

Lord, I'm not doing the wrong thing, am I?

That was probably not a good prayer. His prayer should be more along the lines of, *Lord, show me Your will.* But he hadn't been able to pass up the opportunity of having Sondra all to himself.

"That's probably why you know so much about everything," he said casually, responding to her last statement. There had been a few moments of silence in his truck, which when a person was around Sondra, there wasn't much silence. He didn't mind. He enjoyed listening to her. He liked the tone of her voice. There was something about it that...made him smile. It just seemed to vibrate down through his chest, making him feel warm and happy inside.

"Really? You think I know a lot?"

"Yeah. I haven't heard of a show that you couldn't tell me all about."

"Well... Thanks. I do try to stay up on all the latest." Her smile was pleased and happy, like someone had finally noticed her. "In fact, did you hear about the latest Hollywood couple breaking up?"

"No. You gonna tell me about it?" he asked, even though he was less interested in hearing about a Hollywood breakup than he was in just listening to Sondra talk.

"Well, I certainly can, although I don't believe in cheating."

"No. That seems to be what a lot of the Hollywood people do. They hook up, then they break up. It's like a cycle." He lifted his shoulder. "I think once you get into that cycle, it's kind of hard to break it, because when things don't work out, your automatic answer is to break up."

"Oh. I hadn't ever thought of that." She was quiet for a few moments, like she was thinking about what he said. He felt a little hope bloom in his chest. He had never tried to talk to her about anything, and the idea that she was weighing his words and believing them made him feel a little bolder.

"Isn't that true?" he asked, without really expecting an answer. "When breaking up is the solution to your problems, divorce is the first thing you look at when your marriage doesn't go the way you think it should."

"Well, it's true that there are a lot of Hollywood couples that don't stay together. In fact, I can only name a few who have." And then she started ticking them off on her fingers.

He listened, although he didn't recognize any of the names. He supposed if he spent enough time with her, he would start knowing these people the same way she did. She talked about them like they were her friends. Like she knew them personally. And that was just kind of odd, since to his knowledge, she had never met any of them. It was so weird to think of a complete stranger as someone who was...close to you.

Again, he thought about her upbringing and the fact that she hadn't seemed to have too many people who cared about her, so it maybe was understandable that she got so invested in the lives of people she didn't even know.

Maybe, maybe if he could play his cards right, she could get invested in him.

Sign up for Jessie's newsletter! Get a free book, access to exclusive bonus content, get fun and funny updates on her life on the farm and more!

A Gift from Jessie

View this code through your smart phone camera to be taken to a page where you can download a FREE ebook when you sign up to get updates from Jessie Gussman! Find out why people say, "Jessie's is the only newsletter I open and read" and "You make my day brighter. Love, love, love reading your newsletters. I don't know where you find time to write books. You are so busy living life. A true blessing." and "I know from now on that I can't be drinking my morning coffee while reading your newsletter – I laughed so hard I sprayed it out all over the table!"

Claim your free book from Jessie!